SchoolBoy

Katavious Ellis

STREET CHRONICLES

Ellis

Join us on our social networks
Like us on Facebook
G Street Chronicles Fan Page
G Street Chronicles CEO Exclusive Readers Group

Follow us on Twitter
@GStreetChronicl

$15.00
5/2/14
PC

114001846
JG

schoolBoy

Acknowledgements

As always, I have to begin by giving thanks to God for guiding my life, my career. Without a strong sense of spirituality none of this would have been possible.

Thank you to my mother Jackie Ellis for bringing me into this world and for always supporting me. I hope that you are around for many years to come so I can continue to spoil you.

Also I would like to thank my son Quontaviuos and daughter Shanteria for giving me the motivation I needed to stay focused. Daddy loves y'all!

I would like to give a shout out to my family; Dana Ellis, Antionette Ashby, Briana Sampler, Lil D, Miracle Joe and all my nieces and nephews for there are far too many to name but everyone of you know that I love y'all.

I would like to give special thanks to Marquita Hazelett and sister Detria Sellers for being such a great influence in helping me grow. May God bless you all.

Much love to my G Street family; CEO George Sherman Hudson, VP Shawna A., Author Mz. Robinson, Author V. Brown, Author Fire & Ice, Author BlaQue, Author Sabrina Eubanks, Chandra BG? and everyone one else in the family.

Last but not least I would like to acknowledge a few good men who are behind the wall striving for a change. Qawi Wheeler, Reggie "Reggie Rich Buckhead" Walker, Danavin "Dino" McCoy, Terrance "Goldy" Demons, Demarcus "Jawan" Marshall, Maurice Brown...the world needs y'all brothers.

I dedicate this book to the memory of my lovely sister

Laketa Ellis…Rest In Peace

CHAPTER 1

The sun was brightly shining through the front windshield of Money Mac's Now&Later sky-blue Monte Carlo SS. "No matter what you do in life, always keep education first," young Todd's father told him as he dropped him off in front of West Fulton High School. Money Mac was from the old school. He always felt the need to leave his son with some words of wisdom. He strongly believed in giving back; it was something his own father had instilled in him as a young'n. "You understand what I'm saying, Todd?"

"Yes, sir," Todd responded with a serious look on his face.

Money made a complete stop behind the parked school buses, and Todd quickly reached for the door handle. "Hold up, young pimpin'!" Money Mac demanded.

Todd released his grip of the door, turning his attention to his father.

"I know you're excited to be back at school, which is a great thing, but don't just get out the car without showing some love."

Todd half embraced Money and gave him some dap. Todd viewed his father as one of the best fathers to have ever walked the Earth.

"I love you too. I'll be here to pick you up around 2:30, so please be out front when I pull up."

"Fa sho."

Money looked at his watch. "Okay. Get going before the bell ring."

Todd grabbed his book bag from the floor, then got out of the car.

As soon as Money saw his boy walking through the double doors at the front entrance of the school, he slowly pulled out of the parking lot.

* * *

A fresh scent of some different kind of fragrance filled the crowded hallway of the high school. Everyone seemed excited now that the weekend was over.

"Yo Todd." His best friend Chris walked up and stated with a smile.

Todd smiled back when he saw his good friend. "What up bro?"

West Fulton was one of the most popular schools on the outskirts of Atlanta. Nearly every project, including Hollywood Court, Bankhead Court, Perry Homes, Hollywood Brooks, and many more fed students into the school. There were so many fights at West Fulton that the Atlanta police had to assign officers for hallway duty. Every project had its own crew, but those of high recognition were able to kick it with any crew they wanted.

"After school's out, I'm coming over to play the Xbox," Chris said, standing there with his back against the lockers.

"We can do that. But what you got going on this morning, bro?"

Chris pointed at his backpack that was still slung over his

shoulder. "Trying to get this money up selling all this candy."

Todd placed his book bag in his locker and closed it. "I see. You still at gettin' to the money, huh?"

* * *

Chris and Todd treated each other like brothers. They'd been best friends since first grade. Chris was equipped with unique qualities that had helped him survive as a kid of the projects. He'd grown up in Teachwood projects, and he had no father to show him how to be a man, so most of his knowledge came from watching the drug dealers who hustled day in and day out. When Chris was only three years old, his father Hurricane had been shot to death in one of Atlanta's biggest gambling houses. After finally accepting Hurricane's untimely death, Chris's mother, Ms. Sarah, felt the need to move on with her life. She and Chris moved to Hollywood Court apartments in the hopes of finding a new life. Hollywood Court was a nice apartment complex, with a clean basketball court situated in the middle. There was also a center where kids could go after school. Little did Sarah know that trouble would lie ahead. Unfortunately, the many neighborhood drug dealers caused a great deal of problems while turning the once decent apartments into a bad living area. Still, life was good for Chris and Sarah, until she met a man by the name of Too Sweet at a sports bar out on MLK.

After they'd been dating for nearly two years, Sarah allowed Too Sweet to move in with Chris and her. Not long after that, she became pregnant by Too Sweet, and she stayed home cooking and cleaning while he ran the streets all night. Chris didn't like Too Sweet at all, but he accepted him because of the happiness the man seemed to bring to his mother.

Everything went well until Too Sweet started drinking. He was an angry drunk, and he began beating on Ms. Sarah, even while she was eight months pregnant with his baby girl. Through a best friend, Sarah found out that drinking was not Too Sweet's only bad habit. He was also addicted to crack cocaine. His addiction had gotten so bad that he'd even started taking possessions out of their home to sell—things like Chris's videogames, the television, shoes, food, and the family's living room couch. Sarah hated Too Sweet's habit and what it was doing to him, but after she went into labor and gave birth to their daughter Laketa, she began to smoke crack cocaine herself. Before long, she was hanging out in the streets for weeks on end, while Chris and little Laketa stayed with Mrs. Ruth, the next-door neighbor.

Money Mac lived three doors down from Ms. Sarah's place. One day when he was pulling up to the apartments, he saw Ms. Sarah sitting on the ground crying because she couldn't get any drugs. Money knew the love his son Todd had for Chris, so he got out of the car, picked Ms. Sarah up off the ground, and took her to a rehabilitation program so she could get help. Money began looking after Chris and Laketa with Mrs.Ruth while Sarah worked on getting her life back together for herself and her children. Money became Chris's biggest idol. From time to time he would take Todd and Chris to car shows all around the city because they both loved cars so much.

When Chris was twelve, he started hustling with the boys on the corner, selling dime bags of marijuana. In spite of the good influence of Money Mac when it came to education, Chris was not like Todd, who often kept his head in the books. Money Mac was fully aware of Chris's hustling in Hollywood Courts, but Mrs.Ruth had no knowledge of what he was up to.

* * *

The school bell finally rang for class to begin. Todd and Chris rushed toward the front door so they wouldn't be late for first-period class.

Man, I'm glad this is my last year, Todd thought as he and Chris strolled down the hallway.

From a distance, Todd noticed his girl Monica and her best friend Cristal approaching. Monica and Cristal stopped all movement in the hallway as they walked. They looked like two beautiful Louis Vuitton models. Monica's sky-blue Apple Bottom shirt matched her short cheerleader skirt. She was wearing matching Reebok Classics, blue lip gloss, and blue ankle socks. Her jet-black hair hung over her shoulders and down her back. Cristal was wearing the same thing, except her color of choice was red, and her hair hung long and straight down the center of her back.

At the same time, they both stopped in front of Todd and Chris.

"Hey, boo!" Monica said, looking Todd directly in his light green eyes.

"Hey, baby girl. I see you looking hot," Todd answered, then cut his eyes over at Cristal. He had to admit to himself that she was also very attractive and fine in all the right places.

"Hey, Chris," Cristal said with a smile.

"Hey there sexy, when are you going to let me take you out to the movies?"

Cristal and Monica looked at each other in surprise.

"What? Why you looking at me, girl? He talking to you," Monica said.

Cristal turned back to Chris. "I would, but you know I got a man, Chris, and—"

Cutting her off, Chris said, "Look, Cristal. I am not a hater by far. When he stop treating you right or fulfilling his obligation, get at me."

She began to blush. "Boy, you crazy."

"I'm just real, baby girl. Hey, Todd, I'ma catch up with you at lunchtime, man." Chris locked hands with Todd for a moment before he walked off.

Monica put her arms around Todd's neck. "Baby, yo' dad came over to my house last night," she said softly, kissing his earlobe.

"Girl, you better slow down before you start some in this hallway."

The bell rang again for last call, and the hallway emptied quickly.

"I can finish what I start, but let me get going. Oh yeah… I'm spending the night over at Cristal's house this weekend. Call me."

"Okay. I will, baby girl."

"I love you," Monica said as she kissed Todd on the lips.

"I love you too, my queen. Be easy, Cristal," he said before he ran to class.

"Okay, Todd," Cristal replied.

* * *

"What it do, bro?" Chris said.

"Boy, what's good with you? I been looking all over for you."

"Mr. Hill tried to keep me in that damn classroom until I finished my work."

"That's one teacher here that I hate for real," said Todd.

"I know, right?"

"Let's go sit at that table there," Todd said, nodding to the table next to the exit door.

Todd and Chris took a seat as Monica, Cristal, and Kee-Kee walked up, carrying their trays.

* * *

Kee-Kee was another girl Todd had run through sexually, but he'd not been dealing with her on that level since his friend Hakim had fallen in love with her.

Todd and Hakim had been friends since first grade. Hakim had been in and out of jail a lot and when he was in the mix he and Todd would hang out at My Brother's Keeper (MBK) night spot every Saturday. They often bet $5 on who could get the most phone numbers, and Todd always won. Hakim was fourteen when he was busted for the first time. He had stole an old white lady's Cadillac Escalade from the parking lot of the Lenox Mall. He'd lived his life as a young hustler, a drug dealer who was trying to take care of his six-year-old little sister, Aminah. His mother, Hager, was strung out on heroin so badly that she'd begun to look like one of those walkers from The Walking Dead.

When the judge sentenced Hakim to four years, Ms. Hager died that same week from a heroin overdose. Children's Services planned to take Aminah away, and when they walked into the open front door, they found Hager lying on the couch with a needle still jutting out of her arm. Little Aminah was still sound asleep in her room, and they took her and shipped her off to a foster home while Hakim was getting use to the prison life.

* * *

"What's up, baby?" Monica asked, sitting next to Todd.

"Nothing much."

Chris undressed Kee-Kee with his eyes, but he knew Todd wasn't going to allow him to say an out-of-the-way word to Hakim's woman, so he closed his eyes and dropped his head.

"What's up?" Kee-Kee asked, taking a seat across from him.

"Shit, not much on my end. You heard anything from my boy Hakim yet?" Todd never really understood why Hakim loved Kee-Kee, considering Hakim knew Todd had slept with her numerous times. Kee-Kee was the type of girl who loved to play with guys' hearts, but with Hakim, it was different. She really, truly loved him.

"Yes! My baby only got two more months left."

Todd looked over at Kee-Kee with a smirk on his face.

Monica placed her arm around Todd's neck. "What's wrong, baby boy?"

"I'm good."

"Boo, you gotta come over to Cristal's house this weekend," Monica said, laying her head on Todd's shoulder.

"I'll come when you call."

"Oh shit, girl!" Cristal shouted, looking over Todd's shoulder.

Todd, Monica, Kee-Kee, and Chris turned around at the same time. Monica's ex-boyfriend Meco was entering the cafeteria through the side exit door, followed by his two younger brothers, Rock and AJ.

* * *

Meco, AJ, and Rock were all doped out. The only time they ever came to school was around lunchtime, and then only to start trouble. Meco was considered a straight-out loser, with the mentality of a five-year-old. He was seventeen, and he'd been held back twice. The word on the street was that he and his two brothers were going around robbing drug dealers and corner stores. Their mother didn't care what they did, as long as she had a hit of crack cocaine to satisfy her needs. The three brothers had grown up with multiple men coming in and out of their mother's bedroom, and some nights they went to bed without even a grain of bread in their bellies.

* * *

Meco walked up behind Monica, reached over her shoulder, and grabbed a cookie from her tray. As he began to eat it crumbs fell from his mouth, for he chewed wide and hard, like a stupid animal. "Come here, girl!" Meco demanded, pulling Monica by the arm.

She quickly snatched her arm away. "Boy, leave me the fuck alone!" Monica looked down at Todd, who was still drinking his milk.

Chris gave Todd the damn-bro-what-you-gon'-do eye, but Todd just sat there.

Meco took a bite of Monica's sandwich, then tossed it

back on her tray.

"Boy, don't you see me with my man?"

A smile suddenly appeared on Todd's face, for that was his cue. Money Mac had taught Todd never to check another man until a woman let it be known that she was his property.

Meco looked down at Todd, then over at Chris. "Where he at then? I don't see no man here."

Rock and AJ started laughing out loud, causing everyone in the cafeteria to turn around.

Todd and Chris both remained calm, not saying a word.

"Oh, you talkin' 'bout Todd? Damn. My fault, dawg," Meco said, patting Todd on the top of his head.

Todd jumped to his feet and punched Meco directly in his mouth, causing Meco to fall to the floor like lumber. Todd immediately started kicking Meco in the face with his hard Timberland boots. Soon, blood was flying everywhere.

Rock rushed toward Todd with rage, but he was immediately stopped. Before he could even raise his right fist to defend his brother, Chris punched him from his blind side, right above his temple. Rock's body smashed onto the table violently, sending all the trays and food flying to the floor and splashing milk everywhere.

Most of the kids in the cafeteria began standing on top of the tables, trying to get a better view of the fight. Some stood around, cheering Todd on.

AJ stood in place, clenching his fists tightly, as if he was in a state of shock. He had never seen anyone beat Meco down the way Todd was. He glanced over at his other brother, Rock, who was still trying to recover from the hard blow Chris had given him. "Stop, mother-fucker!" AJ shouted as Todd continued to kick Meco in his back. When AJ saw that

Todd wasn't going to stop beating Meco, he reached into his waistband and pulled out a chrome .357 revolver.

All the kids started running out of the cafeteria when they caught sight of the weapon.

"Yeah! Li'l punk-ass nigga! I said you better stop!" AJ screamed, pointing the pistol sideways at Todd's back.

Todd didn't even hear AJ because he was still in the zone, kicking Meco even more senseless than he naturally was.

"Don't shoot him, AJ!" Monica wailed as tears rolled down her cheeks.

When Todd heard Monica mention the word "shoot," he slowly turned around, only to find himself staring frightfully down the barrel of AJ's .357, pointed directly in his face.

"What now, Todd? You don't look so macho now!" AJ took two steps back, pointing the gun at Todd, then over at Chris, who was standing next to Monica with his fists balled up.

Chris gave AJ a look of death, while Rock helped Meco get off the floor. Blood was gushing from Meco's nose like a crimson waterfall. "So you gon' shoot us or not, pussy-ass nigga?" Chris dared, as if he didn't care if he lived or died.

AJ bit down on his bottom lip and kept his finger on the trigger. "Fuck you!" he said, desperately wanting to let a few rounds off into Chris's body. AJ had never shot anyone before, though, and he was more nervous than Todd and Monica put together.

"FREEZE!" the policeman shouted as he aimed his 9mm Smith & Wesson directly at AJ.

Without turning around, AJ raised his arms in the air. He wasn't willing to take a chance of making the wrong move and getting himself killed. He tossed the pistol, then glanced over to his right.

The policeman was very old, with grayish hair and a pair of Coke-bottle-thick lenses resting atop his wrinkled nose. AJ noticed the Caucasian officer moving in on him at a slow pace, as if something was wrong with his old left leg. He took advantage of the situation and rushed for the side exit door.

The policeman who was supposed to protect the kids in the school didn't even try to chase AJ. He simply picked up the .357, placed his 9mm in his holster, then looked over at Rock and Meco. "Don't move, you two!" the policeman demanded.

Their heads turned toward the policeman at the same time, and they knew there wasn't a second to spare. Meco made a run for the exit, holding his ribs all the way, while Rock trailed behind.

When the officer saw that the cafeteria was safe and secure from the thugs, he walked up to Chris and grabbed him by the forearm. "Come with me young man."

Chris tried to pull away from his grip. "Man, let me the fuck go, old man."

"Sir, he wasn't—" Todd started, but he was cut short when his teacher, Mr. Hill, grabbed him from behind. "Man, what the fuck is wrong with you?" Todd asked angrily.

Mr. Hill didn't respond. Instead, he simply helped the policeman handcuff Chris and Todd and escort them to the principal's office.

In the office, Kee-Kee, Monica, Cristal, and a few other girls from their 'hood were already there, trying to explain how the incident went down.

Principal Wright sat on the edge of his desk with one hand under his chin and the other across his thigh.

Mr. Hill and the policeman shoved Todd and Chris into the office, their hands still cuffed behind their backs.

Mr. Wright told Monica and her friends to head back to class, then took a seat in his black leather office chair that sat behind his desk. "Mr. Jackson, I'm not going to suspend you and Mr. Pue, but what I am going to do is call your father. As for you, Mr. Pue, I will be contacting your guardian. Due to the statements and information I've received from witnesses, I will inform all concerned parents that you two were only trying to protect the other students. I can assure you that Mr. Baker and his two brothers will be brought up on charges."

Yeah, if my dad don't find them first, Todd thought to himself.

Mr. Wright stood and leaned over his desk. "However, if I hear anything else out of you two, I will personally take you down to the Juvenile Detention Center myself. Officer Webster, please release them from their handcuffs. Now, do you two understand the promise I just made?"

"Yes, sir," they answered at the same time.

After they left, Mr. Wright picked up the phone and dialed Todd's father but the call went straight to voicemail.

* * *

After Todd walked Monica to her school bus, he waited with Chris until his foster mother picked him up. Todd spotted Money Mac's white Range Rover pulling into the school parking lot. When Todd got in the truck, Sherri, Star, and Misty were sitting in the back seat, looking like Money had been working them for days. Money's prostitutes didn't care how long they had to stay on the corner selling their bodies.

All they cared about was who could bring in the most money before the day was done.

Money Mac made sure he took good care of his girls. Every three weeks, he rounded them up for checkups at Grady Memorial Clinic. He even bought them the best clothes to wear while they were working their ho stroll.

Money needed to drop his hoes off on Simpson Road, but he'd decided to stop by and pick young Todd up first. He noticed what a mess Todd was. "Boy, why you got fresh blood all over your boots?"

"I got into a fight," Todd calmly responded.

Money started smiling from ear to ear. "Was it over some ho?"

"Nah man. Come on now! You know I don't get down like that!"

Money knew Todd was telling the truth. He just felt the need to test the boy every now and then. "Give me the run-down on what happened."

"Well, I was sitting at the lunch table when this fool Meco walked up behind me and put his hand on my head."

"So you beat him up for touching you?"

"No, Dad. Just listen."

"Okay. Go ahead."

"He's Monica's ex-boyfriend. She checked him, and that was when he put his hand on me. I jumped out of my seat and punched him in the mouth. His brother Rock tried to jump in, but Chris got on him."

"So they was gonna jump you?" Money asked, pulling up at a red light.

"The younger brother, AJ, pulled out a gun," Todd said, knowing Money would get angry.

Money Mac's face immediately formed into a frown. "You mean to tell me somebody pulled a gun on you in school?" he asked, trying to remain calm.

Damn. Why'd I say that? Todd thought to himself. Todd, Sherri, Star, and Misty all knew how Money was when it came to gun play. He instantly stopped the conversation and turned up the Isley Brothers that was softly playing from the truck surround sound system.

Money was burning like flames inside. Money made a right turn into the BP gas station. He saw a group of young drug dealers standing in front of a payphone, having a conversation. Two other dealers sat in a green Infiniti, making a business transaction.

"My main man Money! How 'bout letting me wash your window for a few dollars?" an old black crack fiend asked, standing by the gas pump with a dingy yellow cloth in one hand and a bottle of watered-down glass cleaner in the other.

"Look, BB, get far away from my truck. I just gave you $20 earlier today."

The crack fiend walked over to the black Buick Regal that had just pulled up to another gas pump. Before he could open his mouth, the young man who had just exited the nice car threw his hands up in the air.

"I don't got shit for you old man. Get a job!"

"Say, ho, go put $20 on pump 9," Money ordered Sherri.

* * *

Sherri was a white girl with blonde hair, and she had the face of a super model. She stood about five-six and had a petite frame, around 135 pounds. Her sex appeal allowed her to captivate nearly any man she wanted.

Star, another of Money Mac's hoes, was half-Chinese, half-black, with long, silky black hair, full lips, and a small waist. She stood five-five and would have weighed about the same as Sherri if she were soaking wet.

Misty was a white girl, a redhead, with a beautiful face and a healthy five-eight, 142-pound figure.

Money Mac dressed his girls in white Gucci skirt sets and matching stilettos. They also wore small necklaces around their necks with charms that said, "Money's Ho."

* * *

"And you, ho, go pump my gas," Money said over his shoulder to Star.

Then he turned and said, "Oh yeah…Misty, go grab me some blunts. I need to talk to my son."

Misty, Star, and Sherri carried out his commands without delay.

Once the prostitutes were out of earshot, Money Mac reached in his ashtray, grabbed a rolled-up marijuana blunt, and fired it up. "So what are you gonna do, li'l man?"

"What do you mean?"

"About that nigga who pulled the gun on you," he said, inhaling the weed smoke.

"I'ma beat his ass when I catch up with him." Todd pushed the button to roll down his window.

Money exhaled the smoke. "So you don't want them niggas dead?"

Todd's eyes grew large, and his heart started beating at a tremendously fast rate. He had never known his father to talk in that threatening way—at least not around him. Todd had heard many stories in the 'hood about his father shooting people, but he'd always taken them for rumors. Hearing the words come directly from his father's mouth made him nervous. "It ain't that serious," he said.

"The fuck it ain't!" Money raised his voice to let Todd know just how serious he was.

Todd sat in the passenger seat with his hand laid back on the headrest.

"Listen to me, son. These young niggas is killin' for fun around here, without a fucking excuse. I'm not saying you need to go around shooting people, but you gotta protect yourself, baby. Now can you dig it?"

Todd nodded his head.

"You too beautiful to be fucking up your face, young pimpin'."

"Dad…"

"What's up?"

"Have you ever killed anyone?"

Before responding, Money took a hit of the blunt, then placed it back in the ashtray. He reached under his seat and came up with a black Glock .40. "For you, I'll kill anybody in a heartbeat."

My dad's crazy, Todd thought.

Misty, Star, and Sherri hopped back in the truck, and Money started the engine, then pulled into traffic, with the gun lying in his lap. "Say, Todd, what your pockets look like?" he asked.

Todd started patting his pockets. "I am broker than that crack-head back there at the gas station."

The girls began to laugh and giggle from the back seat.

"Star, what was your tip, ho?"

"It was $500, Daddy."

"Ho, give that to pimpin' Todd."

Without any complaint whatsoever, Star reached into her small Gucci purse and gave Todd the $500 she'd made off the Mexican the night before. Whenever it came to Money or Todd, the girls did whatever it took to make sure they were straight.

"That's yours, so get used to having big banks," Money said to Todd with a smile.

Todd had a big smile of his own on his face as he took the money from Star. He loved his father and admired the power he possessed over women. It was the first time Money Mac had ever allowed his prostitutes to give their tips to Todd. The rules of the pimp game meant hoes were not supposed to ever put their tips in another pimp's hand. Whenever a ho was in the presence of another pimp who was not hers, she was supposed to lower her eyes and stand behind her pimp. Also, if any pimp was able to knock another for his ho, there were no hard feelings. There had to be mad respect and congratulations to the new pimp for pimping so hard. Those were the rules, and Money Mac stood by them.

"Ho, where that tip from?" he asked Star.

"Out my ass, Daddy," Star answered, showing no shame.

"And, ho, how do you feel giving a pimp his money?"

"It feels great, Daddy?"

* * *

Money Mac dropped Star, Sherri, and Misty off on Simpson just as the sun was going down. All the neighborhood kids were out riding their bikes up and down the street.

Todd looked to his right and saw a group of his friends on the field playing football.

Money pulled into the driveway of a beautiful ranch-style stucco house, nestled among eucalyptus trees. He had the house built in Riverdale, Georgia, which was out of the West Fulton district, but he allowed Todd to keep going to school with all of his friends. As long as Money Mac's boy was getting a good education, that was fine with him. "Why don't you like kicking it with your new friends?"

"I do, they cool."

Money Mac parked behind his candy-red Lexus. His sky-blue Monte Carlo SS was parked on the lawn right next to Todd's four-wheeler. "I have to make a run, so don't burn the house down," Money said.

"You tripping. I'm going to sleep," Todd said as he climbed out of the Range Rover.

"Okay. See you later," Money said as he backed out of the driveway.

* * *

The inside of the house was richly decorated and furnished with beautiful green Italian leather furniture. The floors were marble, polished to a high sheen, and a huge built-in aquarium filled with tropical fish created one of the living room walls.

Todd walked through the house, went upstairs and laid down. Minutes later he was fast asleep. The clock on the nightstand read 2:15 a.m when the phone started ringing. Todd was still half-asleep when he rolled to the edge of his California king-sized bed and grabbed the cordless to see who it was. "Hello?" Todd answered.

"Boy, get yo' ass up. I'm on my way to get you!" Money shouted.

"Where are we going, whats up? It's the middle of the night."

"I don't care what time it is! We got business to handle, so stop asking questions and be ready when I pull up."

"Okay. I'll be ready," Todd said, then hung up.

He tossed the phone on the bed, went into the bathroom, and started brushing his teeth. Todd was dressed within minutes, and he decided to grab some orange juice from the refrigerator while he waited, hoping it might wake him up.

For an hour, Todd sat at the kitchen table, replaying in his head how he'd beaten Meco down in front of the whole school. "Damn. Where's—" Todd's words were cut short by the loud sound of Money's truck dual pipes. He placed the empty juice bottle down on the table before he rushed out the front door.

"Boy, get in!" Money Mac yelled from the driver window.

Todd hopped into the back seat of the Range Rover.

* * *

Grip, one of money's right-hand men, was riding shotgun, wearing a pair of sunglasses, and he had a bottle of Hennessy in his right hand. He was five-nine, with very broad shoulders. His hair was low cut, and he had a noticeable gut. He'd grown up with Money Mac in the streets of Atlanta, when pimping was all about Cadillac Fleetwoods, Vogue whitewalls, gold, and hoes—all equal to fat bank rolls. Grip and Money had started their own pimping enterprise, and it grew to a state-to-state enterprise when a pimp by the name of Sir Charles got knocked for prostituting underage girls.

Money's other right-hand man, Mac-9, was sitting in the back seat, puffing on a cigarette, his eyes bloodshot from the marijuana he and Money had smoked earlier. Mac-9 was only five-five, and he had a bald head, thick eyebrows, and a dark complexion, with a few tattoos on his right arm. Mac-9 would put one in the mind of 2Pac, very outspoken and bold when it came to beef, but pimping wasn't Mac-9's thing at all. He loved to kill, sell drugs, and rob big-time dope boys. Mac-9 and Money Mac had grown up together as well.

As teenagers, they'd called themselves "The World-Class 'Recking Crew." Money, Grip, and Mac-9 had one of the most notorious robbing crews around, since the Down by Law gang of the late eighties. Many drug dealers feared Mac-9 and the young crew he kept with him. During the year of 2010, Money Mac shot a man twice in the head for cheating on him in a poker game. Mac-9 took the rap because he felt Money Mac was the true brains for all the business action throughout the streets of Atlanta. Money made sure Mac-9 had the best lawyer that money could buy. After Mac-9 had been locked up for a year in the Fulton County Jail, his attorney, Mr. Franklin, convinced the district attorney to drop the charges, due to lack of evidence.

* * *

"What's good, young blood?" Grip asked, placing a cigarette in his mouth.

Todd looked bewildered. "Nothing much."

Mac-9 greeted Todd with a handshake.

Money Mac turned off the I-20 expressway. When he got to the four-way stop sign, he made a quick right down

Candler Road, drove a bit, then pulled into the driveway of an old, run-down house that sat back in a wooded area. The grass in the front lawn was covered with fallen leaves, empty beer bottles, broken crack pipes, and old pizza boxes filled the front and back porches.

Money turned off the engine and stared at Todd through the rearview mirror. "Let's do this!" Money said.

Grip removed a small padlock from the door of the dilapidated old shed. When the door flew open, Todd stood at the threshold with a shocked expression on his face when he saw who was inside.

Meco, Rock, and AJ were inside, tied to old wooden chairs, with duct tape over their mouths. Tears filled their eyes as they tried to mumble through the tape.

"Dad! What the—?"

Money cut his son's words short. "Boy, I told you how it was going down. I mean, you can fight all yo' life until someone put a bullet in your ass, or you can blow this fake-ass mother-fucker's brains out now!"

Todd wasn't trying to hear what Money Mac was saying. All he wanted to do was go home. He thought about making a run for the door and never looking back, but the voice inside him kept telling him to keep his cool.

"You scared, boy?" Money asked Todd when he saw the sweat rolling down the boy's forehead.

Todd tried to respond, but his lips wouldn't budge, and his feet felt like they were glued to the ground.

Money pulled out a chrome 9mm handgun from his waistband.

"Now I'm…I-I…uh, I'm… Dad, what's up?" Todd struggled to ask. He didn't want to punk out in front of

Money, Grip, and Mac-9. Besides, showing AJ who really held the power felt kind of good.

"Say, Mac-9, take care of this for me. Show young Todd how we really roll in these streets," said Money.

Mac-9 smiled, then walked over to Meco. He stared Meco in the eyes for a second, then pulled a .357 revolver from his back pocket. Mac-9 grabbed Meco by the top of his head, shoved the gun in his face, and pulled the trigger. Meco's head jerked back, and blood and pieces of brain matter and bone splashed all over Mac-9's face and shirt.

At the sight of their brother's murder, AJ and Rock started wiggling and mumbling and crying.

Todd simply stood against the wall with his shirt over his eyes.

Mac-9 then walked over to Rock and shot him once, right in the center of his forehead. Rock's body fell backward, and blood oozed all over the payment.

"Now that's how we roll, son," Money said. "No motherfucker gon' pull a gun on you and live to tell about it. Ya feel me, boy?"

Todd started holding his chest, as if he was having a heart attack.

Money Mac strolled over to Todd and shoved the 9mm into his unwilling hand. "Respect is what we stand on, son. If I let this li'l nigga go, he'll go right to the police or try to get back at you, and I can't have that. Now, can you dig it?"

Todd looked down at the gun, then over at AJ, who was shaking his head and pleading with his eyes, mumbling, "Don't do it, Todd," through the tape. "Please!"

Todd slowly walked toward AJ. With every nerve-racking step he took, he thought about AJ pulling out a gun.

That thought played over and over again in his head as he approached the last remaining brother. Todd aimed the gun at AJ's chest, the word "respect," rolling through his mind over and over again.

CHAPTER 2

Todd quickly jumped out of bed. His eyes searched the dark room. His tank top was damp from the sweat rolling down his back. He glanced over at the small digital alarm clock on his nightstand and saw that it was 5:30 a.m. Todd reached over and clicked on the lamp.

He noticed his roommate stretched out across the hardwood floor, with a shirt over his face. He shook his head and walked into the bathroom. Todd stared at himself in the full-length mirror on the bathroom door.

* * *

That night with Money, Grip, and Mac-9 still replayed in his head every time he fell asleep. Killing AJ was something he'd never forget, but Todd still didn't allow that to hold him back from graduating from high school. It had been a while since those murders in that shed, but the nightmare still haunted him. Todd had yet to tell anyone about what had happened to Meco and his two brothers, but word had gotten around, thanks to a few drug dealers from Cumbellton Road spreading rumors. They'd said Mac-9 had pulled up at Simpson Valley Pool Hall in a black-on-black Chevy Tahoe and demanded that Meco and his two brothers get in. Within weeks, that rumor had spread throughout the West Side of

Atlanta like wildfire.

The Atlanta PD received a tip from an unidentified witness, who stated that they'd seen Mac-9 kidnap the three brothers on the same day when they'd been killed. The lead detective, Sergeant Freddie Hopkins, issued a warrant for Mac-9's arrest. Sergeant Hopkins had told the news reporters that he'd been watching Mac-9 for years, but he'd wanted to wait to bring him in until he thought they had a strong case against him. When the SWAT team kicked in Mac-9's front and back doors, they found him sitting on the couch in the dark, smoking a marijuana blunt.

During Mac-9's first appearance in the courtroom, the grand jury sent down a five-count indictment for the murders of Meco, AJ, and Rock.

Money Mac paid a big-time New York lawyer $80,000 in cash to fly down to Atlanta to represent Mac-9. The district attorney wanted to seek the death penalty because of the premeditated, execution-style murders of three young teens.

Mac-9's trial lasted for three whole months, and the grand jury ultimately found him guilty on three counts of first-degree murder. He received a judgment of three life sentences, plus an additional twenty-five years, to be served in the Georgia Department of Corrections.

As for Money Mac, he was still the same old Money, doing what he did best: pimping from state to state with pimping-ass Grip right by his side.

Todd's high school sweetheart, Monica, started dating Chris—of all people—before she enrolled at Georgia State College.

Hakim had finally gotten out of boot camp and was now selling cocaine, ecstasy, and speed throughout the Hollywood

Court apartments.

Chris had started working at the West End Mall Foot Locker part time, to help care of his newborn son, Wāhid. He'd recently been fired for giving special discounts to customers he knew from the 'hood, selling merchandise out the back door at lower than what the store charged for it. Some of his co-workers found out and told his managers what time he made his sales. The manager left one Friday, then circled back and watched Chris in action behind the store. When he caught Chris making a transaction, he didn't even call the police. He simply told him to pick up his last check, return the company uniform, and never come back.

When Hakim had heard that Chris had gotten fired, he gave Chris a bag of crack cocaine and told him to come up. Hakim didn't want Chris, Monica, and their newborn son to struggle like he and his sister Aminah had. Chris allowed Hakim to name his firstborn Wāhid, "unique" in English.

Hakim still had yet to find his baby sister Aminah, who'd been adopted out to a foster family when she was only six years old. All he knew about her was that a family from Boston had adopted her.

No one had heard from Cristal since she and her mother had moved to Florida.

The only reason Todd had chosen to attend Clark Atlanta College was because his mother, Ms. Jackie, had assured him that it was the best college in Georgia. At first, Todd was going to attend Georgia Tech so he could earn a degree in business management; his dream was to open his own successful upscale nightclub in Atlanta.

* * *

After taking a quick shower, Todd headed back to his room, only to find his roommate sitting on the edge of his bed, with his head in his lap. "What's wrong with you?" Todd asked.

"Dude, I'm good. I just been out all fucking night partying," his roommate responded in a sleepy voice.

Todd climbed back into bed and placed his forearm over his eyes. "You be wildin' out for bein' a white boy."

Richard looked over at Todd. "Dude, you always talking in your sleep. Every time I get in late, I hear you saying something about respect. At first I thought you were talking to me, then I realized you were asleep."

"Man, you look like shit warmed over. You best get you some sleep before class starts. I don't feel like talking about it."

"I'm just trying to look out fool," Richard responded.

Todd didn't respond. He just pulled the bed sheet over his head. He needed his rest because he was about to attend his first college class, and he wanted to make sure he was wide awake and that his brain was ready to soak it all in. A few years, and I'll have that degree, he thought as he drifted off for a quick nap.

* * *

Todd entered his first class ready to learn all there was to know about business. The clock on the wall read 2:30 and the professor was still lecturing. Todd fought hard to stay attentive but had lost out. He had fallen asleep in his first class, with his head on the desk.

A sudden push on his shoulder shook him awake from

his dream.

"Class is over handsome," a soft, seductive voice said lowly.

Todd was astonished when he saw the beautiful girl who was speaking to him. He shook his head and rubbed his eyes, just to make sure he wasn't still dreaming. He smiled when he realized she was real. Todd smiled at her and immediately began gathering his belongings. He wasn't about to let her get away. When he got to the hallway, he looked around, but he saw no sign of her anywhere. He tossed his backpack over his shoulder and began walking. To his right were two adorable black females, standing next to a water fountain, having a conversation. Todd was immediately captivated, and the girl with the blue and white Baby Phat shirt, white capris, and open-toed sandals locked eyes with him.

"Damn, Alexus. You just ain't paying attention to a bitch when she talking to you?" her friend asked.

"Pssh! Girl, that nigga there know he's fine as fuck!" Alexus replied, standing there pigeon-toed as she stared at him.

"I've never seen him around here before, but yeah, he's sexy as fuck, girl. Go over there and say something to him." Pooh pushed Alexus in the back.

"Okay, bitch. Damn! Just stop pushing me."

Todd stood in front of the men's restroom with his backpack over his shoulder, watching the girl approach.

Alexus took very small steps toward him. She was more than beautiful, around five-four and just over 130 pounds, light-skinned, with a dimpled smile and perfectly manicured nails. "Excuse me, handsome," she said when she got within earshot of Todd. I couldn't help but notice you standing over here. You new?"

Todd took a step toward her. "Has anyone ever told you that you're an attractive girl?"

She began to blush. "Oh, boy, stop it. I hear that a lot around here. But I must say, you're the only guy who's ever caught my attention."

"That's a good thing, Ms. Lady. I am new here. Can you show a brother around, because I'm a little lost," Todd lied.

"Yeah, I can do that, but first let me talk to my friend Pooh."

"Bet that!"

She turned to walk away.

"Say, pretty lady, what's your name?"

"Alexus."

"Okay. I'm Todd, by the way."

Pooh was drinking from the water fountain when Alexus walked up behind her and tapped her on the shoulder. Pooh jumped and screamed, "Bitch! You scared me!"

Alexus laughed. "Girl, he want me to show him around."

"Fuck! Then what are you waiting on?" Pooh said, glancing over at Todd. "That nigga know he's sexy as hell."

"I know, right? But, bitch, he's mine for now. Anyway, I love you, girl. I'll see you after class, later."

Pooh gave Alexus a hug. "I love you too. Now bye, girl. Go on and get you some of that!"

Alexus and Todd strolled through the college, conversing like they'd known each other for years. After they'd exchanged numbers, Todd agreed to meet up with her at Starbucks on Ralph David Abernathy, in a predominantly white neighborhood. Todd learned that Alexus was twenty-three years old, originally from Memphis, Tennessee, and she'd moved to Atlanta with her oldest brother. She also informed Todd that she worked part time as an exotic dancer to help pay off her student loan. Todd then told her a little bit about himself before they departed and went their separate ways.

* * *

At 2:50, Todd arrived at his second class. On his way through the door, he spotted the girl who'd waken him up earlier. She was standing next to the glass case containing the college football championship trophy and other awards, having a conversation.

All of the sudden, Todd's cell phone started vibrating on his hip. He unsnapped his cell phone holder clipped to his belt and opened the phone. "Hello?" he answered, walking toward the back exit door."

"Shawty, what's up with you?" asked Hakim.

"Nigga, what's good, bro? This ain't the same number neither."

"Yeah, I know. I had to change it because the wrong nigga got a hold of my old number."

"Who dat, bro?" Todd asked.

"That li'l nigga Hot Boy from Simpson Road. The word on the street is he robbing like a mother-fucker and working as an informant. The nigga call me talking about putting him on a lick."

Todd started laughing into the phone.

"So how you liking the college life?" Hakim asked.

"Brah, it's some bad li'l hoes up here. What you doing later?"

"You already finished with class?"

"Shit, not yet, but I will be in an hour," Todd stated, looking at his Rolex.

"Meet me at the S&T Chinese store when you get out of class.

"I told this li'l ho Alexus I'd meet her at Starbucks." Todd hesitated a moment and thought about it. "Nah, you know what, brah? Fuck her right now. I'll be at the store when class is over."

"You is hell on a bitch, young pimpin'. Be easy, bro. I'll see you in a few."

"Bet that." Todd hung up, then placed his cell phone back in its small leather pouch.

Less than an hour later, class was over. Todd rushed through the crowded hallways. He was trying to make it to his room and drop off his belongings before Hakim made it to S&T Chinese store.

Todd's dorm room door was halfway open, but all the lights were off inside. He slowly pushed the door open and reached for the light switch. When the light came on, he found Richard cuddled up on the floor with a slim, petite black girl. "Oh! Sorry for interrupting, y'all. I just need to grab my car keys off the nightstand," Todd said with a smile.

"You good, dude. Just lock the door behind you."

Todd didn't respond. He just threw his backpack on his bed, grabbed his keys, and walked out the door.

The sun was still at its highest peak, so Todd decided to walk instead of driving his custom-painted blackberry '78 Cutlass Supreme. When he got to the S&T corner store, he saw Hakim pulling into the parking lot in his candy teal blue '87 Buick Regal, listening to Goodie Mob's Still Standing. Hakim's car was equipped fully with a 388ci stroker engine, 750-CFM chromed-out Holley carburetor, chrome side mirrors, bumpers, and headlights, and a red oakwood steering wheel.

Hakim parked five feet from a blue telephone booth, then hopped out. He was dressed in a white t-shirt, black jeans, white Air Forces, a gold Cuban link necklace, and gold-rimmed Nefarious sunglasses. Hakim was twenty-two years old now. He was well built, his 162 pounds stacked nicely on his five-eight frame. He wore his hair in waves around his head like a beehive. He was very dark-skinned and had tattoos all over his arms and neck.

"What's good, pimpin'?" Todd replied, giving Hakim dap.

"Nothing much on my end but getting to the money."

Todd stepped back from Hakim. "Boy, I see the game been good to you," he said, not having seen Hakim since his own graduation party a year earlier.

"I put in a lot of work to get what I got. You need to come fuck with me."

Todd gave Hakim a serious look. "I'll pass on that, bro. The dope game ain't for me. I gotta be the one who makes it out the 'hood the right way."

Hakim lowered his head and stared at the pavement. "I feel you on that, and I can't wait till you get that club up and running." He looked around the parking lot and spotted something he liked. "Damn! Who's that li'l ho over there, shawty?"

Todd turned around to see who Hakim was pointing at. "Oh, her? I don't know. She was standing in the hallway earlier, when you called me. She's fine though."

"I know. I'ma get at her!" Hakim turned in her direction. "Say, li'l mama, can I holler at you for a minute?" he yelled.

She walked straight over to him. "What you want,

Hakim?"

Hakim and Todd looked at each other, surprised that the girl knew who Hakim was.

"Damn, sexy," Hakim said. "How you know me?"

She stood there with her hand on her hip. "Who don't know you? I see you all the time when I'm in Hollywood Court."

"That's what's up! Why you ain't never holler at a nigga?"

"Because I be over at my man's house."

Hakim leaned against the hood of his car. "Who ya nigga, Ms. Lady?"

"Corey."

"That's my people! Shawty and Eric making shit happen with that Money 2 Burn music."

"Yes, my baby's doing his thing," she said with pride.

"Say, shawty, where is that girl who was with you in the hallway earlier?" Todd asked.

"Who you talking about?"

"I don't know her name, but she was wearing a yellow shirt."

"Oh. That's her right there."

Todd and Hakim turned around at the same time and saw the girl who'd woken Todd up in class walking out of the store, munching on a bag of chips.

For the first time in Todd's life, he actually felt butterflies in his stomach. "Bro, that's li'l mama I'm digging," Todd said to Hakim.

"Shawty is bad! What's her name, shawty?" he asked the girl, but then he realized he wasn't being too polite. "Oh, but first, what's yours?"

"I'm Nicki, and her name is Tonya, but everyone calls her

'Beautiful'."

As Beautiful was approaching, she heard Nicki say her name. "What about me?"

"Hey, he just asked me your name."

Beautiful looked at Todd and put her hands on her hips. "Why you asking her about me?"

"Damn, pretty lady! You ain't gotta say it like that."

"For real!" Hakim agreed.

"Hakim, stay out of this."

Hakim removed his sunglasses. "Damn. You know me too?"

"Who don't know you?"

"I know, right? I said the same thing," Nicki replied.

Todd started smiling and shaking his head.

"I wonder how I missed seeing y'all. Man, I gotta tighten up."

"Boy, you know you be too damn busy to be seeing us," Beautiful stated. "Now, back to you. Anytime you wanna know something about me, just ask me—not my friends. I bet you got a woman anyway, lookin' the way you do," she said, looking Todd up and down.

Todd sat on the hood of Hakim's Buick. "I see you like to judge a book by its cover."

"No, playboy. I just know your type, that's all," she said, rolling her neck like a snake.

"My 'type'? Shawty, you can't find another male who could walk in my shoes."

Beautiful stepped closer to Todd, hypnotizing him with her seductive eyes.

When she did, Todd did something his dad had told him never to do: He dropped his head. Money had told Todd,

"Whenever a man drops his head while a woman is staring him in the eyes, it's a sign of weakness, and women hate a weak man. If you do that, son, she'll take advantage of you in a heartbeat." He couldn't help it though, because the warmness of Beautiful's sweet-smelling breath gave him an instant hard-on. When the thought of Money's wise words hit his mind, though, he immediately raised his head and looked Beautiful directly in her light brown eyes. "Why are you looking at me like that?" Todd asked.

"Because I'm trying to see if those are your real eyes."

"Well, anytime you wanna know something about me, just ask me," Todd replied in a joking tone, mocking her earlier words.

Hakim and Nicki started laughing hard when they heard him throwing her line back at her.

"That ain't funny," she snapped.

"The man does have a point," Hakim said, laughing.

Just then, a black and green Lincoln Navigator pulled into the parking lot of the S&T store. "Beautiful, bring yo' ass here!" a deep, angry voice yelled from the passenger window.

Neither Todd nor Hakim could make out who the man was because of the dark tint on the windows.

Beautiful quickly ran to the truck when it stopped.

"Shawty, you got that heat on you?" Todd asked Hakim when he saw the young, muscular man step out of the truck, madly upset.

"I keep that thing on standby," Hakim said, touching his hip.

"Good. Stay on point, just in case this lame start acting up."

Hakim stood to his feet. "You straight, shawty. That's that

nigga MT. He ain't talking about shit on this side of town. She probably getting all that nigga money up out of him."

"That's her nigga, Hakim. He be beating her ass too," Nicki explained.

"Fuck that nigga! Todd, let's ride, shawty."

They both hopped in the Buick Regal. Hakim removed his Smith & Wesson .45 from his waistband and passed it over to Todd, who was in the passenger seat, watching the argument between Beautiful and MT. Hakim turned his music up, then put the gear in reverse.

"Shawty, I'ma get that ho Beautiful from that lame."

"I know you are. Look who your daddy is!" Hakim said with a smile.

"Yeah. Money taught me well. So, that nigga MT getting money?"

Hakim made a right turn down Bankhead and reclined in his seat with one hand on the steering wheel. "MT be pushing shit for them niggas Jay-Bo and GG, and they're buying like twenty bricks or better from your daddy."

Todd smirked. "Yeah, they getting to the money fo' sho. Bro, where is the loud pack? I can smell it in the air."

"Look in that brown paper bag under ya seat."

Todd pulled out the bag and opened it. "Shit, brah! This smell like that good, for real."

"It is that good-good. I can only smoke half a blunt by myself, and you know how I smoke. Money said he got it from California. Roll that shit up. It should be like five blunts in the bag too."

Todd rolled the marijuana into the blunt wrap. I got to take Beautiful from that nigga MT, he thought to himself while grabbing a lighter from the ashtray. He took one hit of the blunt and started coughing. "Here. Get this shit!"

Hakim started laughing. "Shawty, I told you that you can't be hitting this shit like that."

"I know that now!" Todd stated, his throat scratchy and his eyes watery from coughing so hard.

CHAPTER 3

Todd lay sideways, with his head propped up against the window. He stared into the blue sky as if he was spaced out. The marijuana blunt had him lost in deep thought, and his whole childhood played through his head like a movie.

Hakim pulled into Hollywood Court apartments. Kids were running around playing, and the street hustlers sat on the hoods of their cars, drinking beer, smoking weed, and listening to rap music. Everyone seemed to be having a good time in the 'hood, like always. All the teenage girls greeted Todd and Hakim with flirtatious smiles and giggles as they cruised through the 'hood, blasting Jay-Z from the stereo.

"Oh yeah. I forgot to tell you that I saw Money Mac before I picked you up," Hakim said as he parked next to a purple Infiniti Q45.

"Really? I talked to him a couple days ago."

They both got out of the car and headed inside. When Todd stepped in the apartment, he looked around and nodded, giving his approval of how neat and clean Kee-Kee kept the house. The two sofas were plush white leather, and there was a black seventy-six-inch HD plasma-screen TV mounted on the wall. There was a Techwood stereo with four kicker speakers, and a blue chinchilla rug sat in the center of the floor. A full-body photograph of Hakim and Kee-Kee, all hugged up together, was on the wall above one of the sofas.

"Kee-Kee!" Hakim yelled from the bottom of the staircase.

Kee-Kee came strolling out of the kitchen with hot curlers in her hair. Her red skin-tights fit perfectly against her petite frame. "What's up, baby?" She took notice of their visitor and said, "Oh! Hey, Todd! Long time, no see."

"Hey there, sis. It's good to see you too," Todd answered.

"Has Chris called yet?" Hakim asked as he sat on the loveseat.

"Not yet. Baby, I gotta finish this head of mine."

Hakim stared Kee-Kee down. "So you going out with them hoes again?"

"Baby, don't talk like that! And when you start questioning anyway?"

"Girl, you better sit yo' ass down with that. Todd know I will get on your ass."

"Keep me out of it," Todd quickly replied.

Kee-Kee and Hakim had always said and done things to keep each other happy. Sometimes, they even made jokes of one another just to get a laugh. Having fun was their way of showing love to each other.

"I can ask what I want, girl," said Hakim.

"I know you can, daddy."

Hakim looked over at Todd. "Do you want to see me on that NBA Live?"

"Damn right!" Todd replied.

Hakim turned on the PlayStation 3, which was connected to the huge plasma-screen HD television.

Todd sat down, removed the .45 handgun from his

waistband, and placed it between the cushions of the white leather sofa.

Hakim pressed PLAY on the control pad, then reached under the loveseat cushion and pulled out another brown paper bag filled with that good weed.

"Damn, shawty! You got weed stashed everywhere," Todd said.

"Naw, dis Kee-Kee's shit. I just be smoking from it. Say, bro, why won't you get two or three pounds from Money and sell it up at the college? I know all dem hoes smoke up there."

Todd looked toward the ceiling, thinking. "Naw, I can't fuck with it."

"All them mother-fuckers smoke, pimp."

"I know, but my focus is only on getting this degree. You dig?"

"Here nigga. Fire this up." Hakim tossed Todd the lighter and rolled up a blunt.

* * *

By the time they finished getting high and playing the videogame, it was dark outside except for the stars scattered about the sky. Crack-heads and street hustlers entered and exited Hakim's apartment, purchasing ecstasy pills and crack cocaine. Kee-Kee handled all the crack cocaine customers who came in and out, while Hakim sold the ecstasy pills.

When Hakim and a few other drug dealers started a game of craps right in the center of the living room, Todd posted up against the wall with Hakim's .45 in his waistband. He wanted to watch Hakim's back just in case someone wanted to act crazy. Todd was well aware of the fact that in the 'hood, when a man's getting that check up, makin' money, everyone could become a potential hater. He and Hakim had vowed to always watch one another's back, no matter what.

Once Todd was sure Hakim was safe, he decided to step outside to get some fresh air. "I see y'all out here getting fucked up on that Hennessy and Rémy," he said to Kee-Kee and her girlfriend Meyon, who were sitting on the front porch, drinking straight out of their bottles.

"Hell yeah, Todd! You already know a bitch gotta get hers in. Shit, nigga. You may have to give me some of that good dick," Meyon said drunkenly, licking the rim of the Rémy bottle.

Todd didn't find Meyon attractive at all. She'd liked him since they were kids, but he'd never paid her any mind. She was about five-three, heavyset, with short hair. She always dressed neatly, but she just wasn't Todd's type.

While Kee-Kee stood on the sidewalk, selling two crack-heads dime bags, Meyon stood up and started rolling her hips and upper body like a belly-dancer.

Todd looked at her and dropped his head. "You need to sit back down, Meyon. I don't wanna see all that."

Meyon ignored Todd and kept right on dancing to the music blasting from the Techwood kickers in the apartment. "Whatever, nigga!" she shouted.

Todd noticed a black Benz with dark tinted windows pulling in, and it parked directly in front of Hakim's apartment. He immediately reached for the .45 under his shirt.

When the window of the Benz rolled down, Money hung his head out the driver window.

"Damn, man! I was gonna fire your ass up, coming up through here like that," Todd yelled from the porch, his hand still gripping the tool. He was relieved to see it was Money and not some money-hungry fool coming through trying to rob.

Money Mac honked the horn twice, and Todd made his way over to the car.

"What's good, Dad?" Todd asked, leaning into the window.

"Nothing much, son. What was you saying on the porch? I had the music up."

Todd smiled. "Naw, you and Grip pulling in here all slow and shit look like the robbing crew."

Money looked over at Grip, who was lying back in the passenger seat, smoking a Newport. "Robbing crew? Boy, if we were the robbing crew, you'da been dead before we pulled up. What? Hakim got niggas wanting to rob him now?" Money calmly asked.

"He was telling me earlier about Hot Boy calling his pone. He had to change his number."

"That's why I couldn't get in touch with his li'l ass. Hakim did right by changing his number, because that young nigga Hot Boy gon' make someone kill his li'l ass for real. But anyway, how is college coming along?"

"Oh, hell yeah! I'm feeling it. There're a lot of hoes lookin' for a pimp."

Money gave Grip some dap. "Now that's pimping!" said Money.

"I see you done got a new Benz."

"Yeah, I got it from a nigga who didn't pay me all my money. When he pay up, then he'll get his car back. Meantime, I'm puttin' some miles on this shit."

Todd grinned. "I see. What's good with you, Grip? You all

over there pimped back and shit."

Grip reached over Money and gave Todd a handshake. "What it do, young blood? You already know on my end, it's the some pimpin' and some mo' pimping."

"I dig that there."

"Where is Hakim?" Money asked.

"Shit! Shawty in the house breaking them niggas on the dice. Want me to go get him for you?"

"Naw, you good. Get in right quick."

Todd hopped in the back seat, and Grip passed him a blunt rolled with marijuana. "You got a lighter on you?" Todd asked.

Grip pushed the car lighter in. "I got you right here. Fire that good shit up."

Money looked back at Todd through the rearview mirror. "So what are you gonna do once you get your degree, my boy?" Money asked curiously.

"I want to get me a ho business started," Todd replied jokingly.

Money gave him a disapproving look.

"Naw, man, I'm just bull-shitting. I want to get my own nightclub up and running—all legit'."

"That's what's up! Look, I got the money for you to start one. Just get your degree. Me and Grip have been working on getting Mac-9 an appeal so we can get his ass out."

"How is he holding up in there?"

"You know Mac-9's a soldier anywhere he go." Even though Todd was only twenty-one years old, Money still felt the need to keep his son on point, ready for the world.

Listen, Todd. Always remember we live by the code of honor. Loyalty isn't just a word. It's an action that manifests itself through your actions. My blood runs through your veins, meaning we don't give in nor give up to anyone. Now, can you dig that?"

"Damn right I dig that."

"How much money you got on you, Todd?" Money asked.

"Just $500."

Money reached into his front pants pocket and pulled out a bankroll of $100 bills, folded in half, with a rubber band around them. "Here. Take this stack. It's just a li'l somethin' to have in your pocket."

"Appreciate ya."

"You don't ever have to thank me. What I got, you got. Me and Grip going out of town for a few days. I need you to hold the house down until we get back."

Todd laid his head back on the headrest. "I got you. What about Princess?" Todd asked, referring to Money's pit bull.

"Oh shit. I can't forget about her! Stop by PetSmart and grab that good-quality Iam's shit for my girl. And tell Hakim to get at me later. Me and Grip probably gon' stop by the pool hall and have a few drinks."

"Okay. When are you all heading out?"

"Sometime this week. I'll let you know before we do."

Todd gave Money and Grip some dap before he hopped out of the Benz and went back inside Hakim's place.

CHAPTER 4

Hakim dropped Todd off on the college campus, then went to the pool hall to meet up with Money Mac and Grip.

When Todd got back to his room, he took a quick shower, then laid back on the bed with a towel wrapped around his waist and his left hand on his chest. He stared at the ceiling as thoughts of Beautiful swirling into his fantasies, until he dozed off to sleep.

A while later, Richard came strutting through the front door smelling like an alcohol factory. He was so drunk that he fell right in front of the small nightstand next to Todd's bed.

The alarm clock eventually woke Todd from his sleep. He stood to his feet and stretched his arms toward the ceiling. "What the fuck?" he said when he saw Richard lying on the floor in a curled-up fetal position. "Man, white boys crazy as fuck," Todd mumbled to himself.

The birds outside the window created a beautiful sound of harmony with their chirping as Todd looked over at the clock. It was 9:15 a.m., and there was only a half-hour till class started. Todd rushed to the shower and made it quick because he wanted to stop by McDonald's for his favorite breakfast sandwich and an orange juice on his way to class.

He pulled into the parking lot of the Golden Arches and

next to a bluish-gray Jeep Wrangler. He could see through the windows of the restaurant that the line inside wasn't very long, so he decided to go in.

Three beautiful girls stared Todd down as they made their way through the double doors. They stood in front of Todd in line, and after they placed their orders and picked up their breakfast, they took a seat at a table near the restrooms.

Todd stepped up to the cashier and placed his order for a breakfast meal. As he did, he heard a soft voice from behind him.

"Hey, Todd," she said.

Todd turned around and saw Ilana smiling at him, a girl he knew from way back at Fulton, since their middle school days. His eyebrows rose. "Damn, girl. What's up? I mean… how you been?"

Ilana blushed. "I been good—just taking care of my son. He's three now."

"I feel that," Todd replied, giving her a hug.

All of the sudden, Beautiful and two other girls came walking through the doors, caught up in conversation. The few guys in the restaurant, whether they were seated or in line or working behind the counter, stared at the girls with lust in their eyes. The females, on the other hand, stared Beautiful and her friends down with envy in their eyes.

Todd kept talking to Ilana, but he couldn't help glimpsing over at Beautiful, admiring her smooth skin, freshly manicured nails, and petite frame.

"I'll see you around, Todd," Ilana said with a frown, noticing that Todd's attention wasn't on her at all.

Todd looked Ilana in the eyes. "I'll catch up with you sometime. Be easy."

Beautiful stepped in front of Todd to place her order.

"Excuse me!" Todd said, tapping her on the shoulder.

She turned around with a smile on her face. "Yes? What's the problem?"

"So you can't speak to a nigga you know?"

"No I can't. Let me finish ordering my food please," she said, rolling her eyes.

Todd took his drink and walked off, then took a seat at an empty table that offered a view of the parking lot.

"May I sit with you?"

Todd looked up and saw Beautiful standing right before him, with her hands on her hips. He quickly jumped to his feet. "Here…take my seat," he said with excitement.

"So I see you're a gentleman."

"Someone's gotta be. There ain't many real men standing nowadays."

Beautiful sat down, then slid toward the window so Todd could sit beside her.

Todd admired all of Beautiful's characteristics, from her short, Kelly Price hairstyle to her 135-pound, petite frame. He even liked the fact that she was playing hard-to-get. Beautiful was twenty-three years old and stood around five-six, and she had a beautiful set of bedroom eyes.

"Excuse me, sir. Your food is ready," the cashier yelled from behind the counter, interrupting them.

"Give me a minute," Todd said to Beautiful, then rushed over to pick up his bag of breakfast to-go.

Beautiful's two girlfriends made their way over to the table, sipping on orange juice.

Todd strolled back to the table with his breakfast. "Look, baby girl, I gotta get going before my class starts. I guess I'll talk to you later…at school."

Beautiful and her two friends looked up at Todd. "That's fine with me," she said.

Todd exited the restaurant without saying another word, feeling like he had Beautiful right where he wanted her.

Beautiful wasn't expecting Todd to just leave like that, so she got up from the table and ran behind him. "Wait a minute, Todd!" she yelled.

Todd turned around quickly, with a surprised look on his face. He set his food in the passenger seat. "What's good, baby girl?" he asked with a serious look on his face.

She stepped really close to him. "I just have one question."

"What's up?"

"I just want to know what it is that you want from me. And be honest with me."

He smiled. "To be real with you, I see something great within you that makes me smile every time I lay eyes on you."

Beautiful's eyes shifted to the pavement, then back up to Todd. "Wow. I've never had a man come at me like that. Most guys only want to get between my legs. Are you for real about what you're saying?"

Todd grabbed Beautiful by the hand. "I liked you the first time I laid eyes on you. Even if I could only have you as a friend, that would be cool."

They both smiled.

"Well, that's all I wanted to know," she said before she turned to go back inside to eat with her friends.

"Beautiful!" Todd yelled.

She turned around while one hand was still gripping the door handle. "Yes, Todd?"

"Do you love MT?"

"Not anymore."

Yes! Todd's thoughts cried out.

"Hold on for a minute. Let me grab my food." She walked into the restaurant, and within minutes, Beautiful and her two friends came walking out with their breakfast all bagged up. Beautiful handed her food to her friend, then walked over to Todd, who was now sitting on the hood of the car. "Thanks for waiting on me. Here's my number. Call me tonight," she said, giving Todd a napkin with her cell number on it.

"I'll be calling you. See you soon, baby girl," he said, keeping a straight face, though he was in utter disbelief with the progress he'd made; just the day before, the girl had been acting like she was all that.

* * *

Todd pulled into the Clark Atlanta parking lot. Some students were walking around the campus, while others were reading, and some were even lying under the trees, staring at their laptops and studying. Todd looked at his watch and saw he only had four minutes to get to class. He took a bite of his hot, buttery biscuit just as his cell phone rang. "What it do?" he answered, a bit irritated and still trying to chew.

"Hey, Todd."

Todd didn't recognize the number, so he asked, "Who's this?"

"Alexus—the girl who showed you around yesterday."

"Oh, yeah! What's up, ma?"

"I waited for you at Starbucks, but you never showed. What happened?"

"I had some shit to handle, but I'll make it up to you. I'll be free Sunday, if that's cool with you."

"That's fine with me. What will we do?"

"I can't tell you just yet. You'll have to wait and see," he stated.

"Okay. I'll call you later. My class is getting ready to start."

Todd looked at the clock on his car radio. "Yeah, mines too."

"Bye, Todd."

He hung up without responding, then quickly ate the rest of his breakfast and headed inside for class.

* * *

Beautiful and her two girlfriends parked right next to Todd's Cutlass.

"Girl, MT gon' kill that nigga if he ever find out you cheating on him," said Beautiful's friend Le Le.

"Girl, fuck him! I ain't fucking with dude no more. He's too fucking demanding for me—not to mention how he hit on me."

Le Le and Peaches started laughing, and Le Le said, "Come on now, Beautiful. How many times have we heard that line, Peaches?"

"A million and one."

Beautiful got upset at her friends for doubting and teasing her. "Bitch, fuck y'all hoes! I'ma leave his ass for real this time."

And with that, they all got out the car and headed for class.

"We'll see when the time comes," said Peaches before they went their separate ways.

"I'll see y'all later!" Beautiful yelled. She knew, deep down inside, that her friends were speaking the truth. Every time she and MT had an argument or disagreement about a matter, she'd leave him for a few days, then go running right back to him when times got hard.

MT had cheated on Beautiful numerous times, and she knew it, yet her love for him just wouldn't allow her to leave him for good.

This time felt different though. Beautiful was actually fed up with MT talking to her any kind of way whenever he was around his boys. Besides, she already liked Todd, and she wanted to give him a chance to be in her life.

When Beautiful had first moved from Miami to Atlanta, MT had met her at the Lenox Mall movie theater while he was taking his kid sister to see Kung Fu Panda. MT had spotted Beautiful standing by the popcorn stand, and he'd been immediately captivated by her slightly slanted eyes, which made her look half-Asian. MT had quickly handed his kid sister Jamilla a $100 bill with his cell phone number on it and told her to give it to Beautiful.

After they'd dated for six months, MT was to the point of giving Beautiful anything and everything she wanted: shoes, clothes, cars, rings, necklaces, and anything else. When they started having sex on a regular basis, though, MT changed for the worse. He began beating on her in front of his friends, and sometimes he even made her stay in his house under lock and key, not allowing her any communication with the outside world.

* * *

Once class was over for the day, Beautiful ran straight to

her dormitory to change shoes, because her boots had gotten too hot for her feet. As soon as she opened her door, the phone started ringing. She grabbed the cordless phone off the charger and answered, "Hello?" without even bothering to look at the caller ID.

"Tonya, baby." It was MT.

Beautiful took a deep breath, then exhaled. "What do you want, MT? I told you it's over with for you and me."

"Baby, please give me a chance."

Tears filled her eyes. "Hell naw, nigga. You put your hands on me for the last time. Live your life with your boys!" She hung up the phone, then sat on the edge of the bed, crying.

CHAPTER 5

Beautiful stood to her feet and slowly made her way to the restroom. She looked at herself in the mirror. The black eyeliner was smeared down her cheeks like a wet painting. She grabbed a piece of toilet paper from the roll and wiped it away. "Why am I crying about this nigga? Beautiful, girl, get yourself together," she said to her reflection, trying to comfort herself.

After Beautiful got herself together, she decided to take a stroll around the campus.

Suddenly, MT pulled into the Clark Atlanta parking lot. "Yeah, bitch, you thought you was gonna get away that fast?" he said when he saw Beautiful exiting her dormitory. He hopped out of his pearl-white Chevrolet Suburban and grabbed Beautiful by her forearm.

She tried to pull free from his grip, but he was too strong. "No, MT! Let me go! I can't do this shit no more," she said, not even believing she was finally standing up to MT.

"Come on, girl. Get your ass in the truck and stop playing with me!" he demanded.

Beautiful snatched her arm away, nearly stumbling over her own two feet. "Look, nigga! You almost made me fall. I'm for real. This time, it's over."

MT slightly bit down on his bottom lip. "Why you don't

want me?" he asked.

"I am not feeling this anymore. You can be with one of your other li'l hoes."

He looked around to see if anyone was looking, but no one was paying them any mind. "I know what's going on. You been fucking that li'l bitch-ass nigga I saw you talking to yesterday at the store."

She took a step back. "What I look like, a ho? Nigga, you the one swinging dick everywhere. Just respect the fact that I do not want you."

MT dropped his head, then looked back up at Beautiful. A tear fell from his right eye, and then he grabbed her by the neck.

She struggled to pull away from his powerful grip, but he overpowered her. "You're hurting me!" she screamed.

MT saw that her eyes were beginning to tear up and her face was turning red. He loosened his grip just enough to give her a little air. "Bitch, take off all those jewels I bought you before I break yo' fucking neck!" he strongly demanded before letting her go.

Beautiful fell to her knees, gasping for air, and tears filled her eyes.

MT looked around. All the students had stopped whatever they were doing and were now staring him down. Some even had their phones out, taking video and pictures of the dramatic scene. MT jerked the necklace from around her neck, then backhanded her in the mouth. Blood flew from Beautiful's nose and mouth as her head jerked backward.

Beautiful lay on the pavement, struggling to remain conscious.

"Man, what the fuck is with you, hitting a girl like that?"

a young, muscular football player said, shoving MT from the back.

MT reached under his shirt and pulled out a black Glock .40, causing the jock to take a few steps back with his hands up. MT smiled broadly. "Fuck, boy, if you ever put your hands on me again, I will heat your ass up."

"Hold up, brah. No one gotta get hurt out here," said the football player.

MT shook his head, then frowned. "Yo, li'l bitch ass ain't even worth me going to jail for," he said before he slowly lowered the pistol.

The football player felt incredibly relieved when he saw MT jump in his truck and speed off, leaving nothing more than a trail of smoke behind him.

Le Le walked out of her dormitory and saw two men helping Beautiful up from the ground. "Oh, hell naw!" Le Le replied, running to her best friend's aid. "Thanks, y'all, but I got her."

The two men placed Beautiful's arm around Le Le's neck.

"What happened, girl?" she asked, escorting Beautiful through the hallway.

"MT jumped on me."

"Do you need to go to the hospital?"

"No way, girl! I'm a soldier."

They both laughed, even though nothing there wasn't much funny about it.

* * *

Todd circled the parking lot of the West End Mall, looking for a place to park. He wanted a vacant spot near the front entrance, right next to the small security booth. There were always young thugs hanging around the mall parking lot, looking for cars to steal, so Todd wasn't taking any chances. He wasn't going to go out like that. Just as his luck would have it, he spotted a white '96 Impala pulling out of the parking lot, and Todd immediately pulled in to that space.

Todd locked his car doors, then made his way into the mall. The bowling ball-marble floor was heavily polished, and three jewelry kiosks and one bookstore were situated in the center. The music store was packed with teenage boys and girls buying the latest Young Jeezy CD. A group of girls in their mid-twenties stood in front of RadioShack, eating ice cream and admiring each other's freshly done manicures.

Foot Locker wasn't that packed, so Todd went inside to buy a pair of black Nike Air Force 1 shoes. Todd then walked through the mall for another forty-five minutes, but he didn't find anything else he wanted. "Let me get out this damn mall. I shoulda went to the Lenox Mall," he mumbled to himself as he strolled through the glass doors with his Foot Locker bag in his hand.

"I know that ain't Todd!" a soft voice said from behind.

Todd turned around, and his mouth dropped wide open. "Oh shit! Tell me I'm dreamin'!"

"No, you're not dreaming, Todd. It's me," Cristal happily replied with a big smile that showed all her teeth. Cristal's honey-colored skin matched the brown sundress she was wearing, and her light brown eyes blended in with the wood-en-bead African necklace that hung from her neck.

Todd couldn't help admiring her new look. "Damn! Nigga ain't get a hug?"

Cristal quickly embraced Todd. "It's been a long time

since I've seen you, boy."

Todd stepped back to take in her beauty. "Yeah, it's been a while. Where you been?"

"Nashville, Tennessee—at college. I came back to Atlanta to enroll at Georgia Tech. I'm trying to get my degree in computer design. I got a new job at Micro-Center, selling computers."

"Well, congratulations! I'm so happy to see that you're doin' good, girl."

"Thank you, Todd. I see you've grown all up over the years. Look at you with your muscles all big."

Todd grinned.

"So, Todd, tell me…what are you doing nowadays?" she asked with a serious expression on her face.

"I go to Clark Atlanta College. I'm trying to get my degree in business management."

"Wow! I knew you were gonna make something of yourself. What about your boys? How are they holding up?"

"Selling drugs, runnin' the streets. Chris was working at that Foot Locker right there, but he got fired for selling shoes out the back door."

Cristal burst out in laughter. "That boy is still crazy, I see," she said.

"Hakim and Monica just had a son."

Cristal placed her hand over her mouth, and a look of surprise came over her face. "For real?"

"How many do you have?"

"What are you talking about? Kids?"

Todd nodded his head. "Uh-huh," he said.

"Boy, I'm saving myself for the right one. What about you? Do you have any?"

"I don't have none at the time."

"Are you for real?"

"Yes. Do you have a man, baby girl?"

Cristal lowered her head. "I am seeing someone, but it's nothing major."

Todd removed his cell phone from the small leather pouch that was connected to his belt. "Give me your number so we can get together."

Cristal retrieved a small card from her purse. "Here. Take this. I had these business cards made up because I'm also working out of my house. I do software updates on computers and phones."

Todd placed his Foot Locker bag on the ground. "I know exactly where you live. What made you move all the way out to Sandy Spring?" he asked, reading the address off the card.

She took a deep breath and smiled. "I just didn't want to live around ignorant-ass black people who prey on your downfalls."

"I can dig that. Look…peep the move, baby girl. There's a party tonight in Teachwood, right by your college. You gotta come."

"I'll damn sure try to be there."

"Well, I won't keep holding you up. Give me another hug," Todd said.

Cristal rapped her arms around Todd's neck like she was getting ready to kiss him on the mouth. When Todd went along with her and grabbed her by the waist, then stared into her light brown eyes, Cristal felt his dick against her stomach. She slowly eased away from his grip. "I want you to know that I've always liked you—since back in middle school," she confessed, then walked back into the mall.

Todd stood at the glass doors lusting after the sight of Cristal's seductive gait. He wished he'd given Cristal a chance in middle school instead of Monica. When she glanced back at him and waved, he allowed his thoughts to run wild. Damn! That girl know she still got it in all the right places.

* * *

Todd cleared his mind and made his way through the parking lot. A group of Nation of Islam men stood in front of the West End Train Station, selling bean pies, fruits, and Final Call newspapers. The skies were filled with clouds, but the sun was shining brightly.

Todd finally stopped walking when he reached the place where his car was supposed to be. He dropped his Foot Locker bag on the pavement and stared at the empty space. His car was gone, and all that was left was some broken glass, scattered on the asphalt.

"Man, this is some fucked up shit!" Todd shouted. He looked around the parking lot and saw the heavyset security guard standing by the post office, talking to a young black girl who was dressed in a beige pantsuit and heels. She had a fresh manicure and long, jet-black hair that hung over her shoulders.

Todd dialed Money's cell number from his touch-screen iPhone.

"Hello?" Money Mac answered on the first ring.

"Dad, somebody just stole my car from the West End Mall parking lot."

"Well, report it. I mean, what do you want me to do about it? Me and Grip is on our way out the door."

Todd's face formed into a frown. "So you can't come pick me up?"

"I got to get going, because we got a long ride. I'll tell you what though. Call Hakim and tell him to bring you to the house. The keys to the Benz will be on the mantel above the fireplace. Just drive that until I get back in town."

A sudden smile appeared on Todd's face. "Check that. I will take good care of it."

"Don't trip it. Just maintain until we get back."

"You already know that," Todd said. "I'll see you when you get home."

After Todd hung up with his dad, he called Hakim, who picked up on the second ring. "What's good, brah?" Hakim asked when he saw Todd's name pop up on his screen.

The music in the background was so loud that Todd could hardly hear. "Turn that radio down for a minute," Todd said.

Hakim obliged Todd's request. "Shawty, what's up?"

"I need you to come get me."

"Where's your ride at, brah?"

Todd took a deep breath before speaking. "Shawty, somebody just stole my shit while I was in the mall buying some shoes."

Hakim burst out in laughter. "Damn, shawty. That's fucked up. I'm on the way. Just hold tight."

* * *

The thick marijuana smoke seeped through the crack in the window as Money and Grip coasted down the 285 Expressway in his SS Monte Carlo.

"A pimping somebody stole Todd's car from the West

End Mall," Money said as he reclined back in the driver seat with one hand on the steering wheel.

"That boy should've had an alarm. Them young niggas be out looking for them old-school cars," Grip said, inhaling the weed smoke from his mouth to his nose.

"It's all good. When we get back, I'ma buy him that new yellow Chevy Camaro SS we seen at the lot the other day."

"They really gon' hate when he pull up in that motherfucker. These young niggas out here with that gang shit gon' think Todd really getting to the money, and they gonna try him up."

Money grabbed the blunt from Grip. "I seriously doubt that. Hakim and Chris got some goons on that Martin Luther King spot that no young nigga wanna see na'on day of."

"Fo sho!"

"Now, if Todd ever start fucking with these streets, he is going to have to make niggas respect him—not because I'm his dad, but because he's a real nigga his damn self."

Grip leaned his head against the window, looking up at the many stars that filled the sky. "Say, pimpin', did you call GG and Jay-Bo?"

Money flicked the ashes from the blunt out the window. "Damn! I knew I forgot something. Todd threw me off when he called me earlier."

Grip retrieved his cell phone from the glove compartment and called GG.

"What's the move?" GG answered, looking at his caller ID.

"Can you still meet us at the same warehouse as before?"

"Hell yeah. Me and Jay-Bo just sitting here having a few drinks.

"Okay. Y'all need to be leaving out like now, with a clear head. You never know how these New York cats may act," he replied calmly.

"We leaving right now, as we speak."

"That's a bet. See y'all there." Grip closed his flip-phone and reclined back in the passenger seat. He looked over at Money. "They leaving out now, pimpin'."

Money inhaled the weed smoke, then passed it to Grip. "Check that."

* * *

GG and Jay-Bo were two of the most feared brothers in Atlanta. They had the West Side on lock with the marijuana and cocaine that Money supplied them. Whenever Money Mac and Grip went to New York for a business transaction, they always asked those two brothers to trail behind, just in case things got out of hand. Jay-Bo and GG pushed six kilos of cocaine a week for Money and Grip on a slow day. Everyone in the streets thought the two brothers were the kingpins of Atlanta, but little did they know that Money and Grip were the brains behind the whole operation. They used their pimpin' skills to keep a low profile so the feds wouldn't be focused on them if it came down to that.

During the summer of 2001, federal agents had raided one of Jay-Bo's main crack houses over on Sells Avenue in Atlanta. Jay-Bo just so happened to be at the house, picking up $200,000 in cash from his workers. FBI agents kicked the front and back doors in, making it impossible for anyone to get away. One federal agent was working undercover, disguised as a drug dealer. He stood before Jay-Bo with his badge around his neck and a stack of indictments in his hand. He had been buying three kilos every two weeks from one of Jay-Bo's workers. When the feds searched the house, they found three kilos of uncooked cocaine inside a DVD player, twelve AK-47 assault rifles in the upstairs closet, and the $200,000 in Jay-Bo's suitcase.

When the case went before Federal Judge Hill, he sentenced Jay-Bo to ten years in the federal penitentiary for money laundering. The three workers pleaded guilty for the three kilos of cocaine and twelve assault rifles, willing to do twenty-five years a piece just to keep Jay-Bo from receiving a life sentence. The young federal agent who'd disguised himself as a drug dealer tried to get the workers to testify against Jay-Bo in exchange for a lighter sentence, but they all refused; they knew GG would have had them killed in or outside of prison if they'd taken a deal. GG went broke helping his brother get the finest lawyer money could buy, so Money pitched in $80,000 to help out with getting a great appeals lawyer for Jay-Bo.

Grip introduced GG to an attorney he knew from New York. Mr. Franklin was one a top-of-the-line federal appeals lawyer, one of the most renowned in the world, hired by the likes of rapper 50 Cent and Lil Boosie and real estate tycoon Donald Trump. Money and Grip trusted him and had even paid him to work on Mac-9's appeal.

* * *

Hakim came speeding through the parking lot with his music blaring loudly. Todd had been waiting in the Best Pizza restaurant for an hour, and he was really angry at Hakim.

When his phone started ringing, he answered, "What's up, brah?" with attitude.

"I'm out here in the parking lot waiting."

Their conversation was interrupted by a young Hispanic waitress, who looked to be in her early twenties. She excused herself to set Todd's pizza down on the wooden table. "Anything else, sir?" she asked politely.

Todd placed his hand over the receiver. "That will be it, pretty lady." He smiled flirtatiously, then walked off. "I'm comin' out of Best Pizza now," he said, reaching into his pocket and placing a $10 bill on the table for a tip.

"Okay," Hakim said, then hung up.

Todd grabbed his box of pizza and his Foot Locker bag and headed for the door that led to the parking lot. He spotted Hakim's Cutlass parked under a light pole in the north end of the parking lot.

As Todd approached the car, he noticed a female sitting in the back seat. When he opened the passenger door to get in, his eyes shot toward the back seat out of curiosity. While her face looked familiar, Todd couldn't make out where he knew her from. "Put this back there," he said, passing his pizza and his new shoes to the girl in the back seat.

She stared at Todd, astonished. "Do you remember me?" she asked.

Todd turned and looked her over. "Hmm. You look familiar, but to be real with you, I can't remember where I seen you at."

"Hell, I'm Beautiful's friend. I seen you at the McDonald's this morning when I was with her."

Todd snapped his fingers, then pointed at the girl. "I knew you looked familiar! What they call you?"

"My name's Peaches."

"That's what's up." Todd turned around and gave Hakim some dap. "Brah, you had me waiting on you for an hour or so."

Hakim smirked, then turned the key in the ignition. "I had to make a few stops. I been tellin' you to get an alarm on that car. Shawty, yo' shit was too clean to not have one."

"I know, shawty. I parked my shit close to the security booth, thinking that fat-ass fuck nigga was gon' be on point with doing his job. I come out the mall and he was standing in front of the post office, trying to spit some game."

Hakim shook his head. "Damn, shawty!" he replied, driving through the late-night traffic.

"I hope the family of the nigga who got my shit has insurance on him."

Peaches couldn't help but overhear their conversation, so she tried to change the subject. "Todd, Beautiful got beat up earlier," she replied softly.

"Who beat her up?" Todd asked, grinning from ear to ear.

"MT! He slapped her to the ground in front of the whole school."

Hakim hooted with laughter

Peaches thumped him on the shoulder. "That shit ain't funny."

"Lil mama, sit your ass back before we wreck."

"Stop laughing at my friend. She got beaten up because of Todd!"

Todd's eyebrows rose. "How in the hell did I get her beat up?"

"She broke up with him…for you."

"For real? Where she at now?" he asked, feeling excitement.

"When I left, she was lying down in her room."

"Brah, take me to Money's house."

"Wait…you know Money Mac?" Peaches asked, shocked.

Todd gave her a weird face. "He's my dad. Why you asking?"

"No reason at all. I remember he was fucking with my old boyfriend on some work."

"That's what's up."

Hakim turned off on the expressway for Riverdale Road.

"I know y'all going to the party tonight," Todd said.

"Where at?"

"Shawty, that boy Li'l Tay just got out the pen from serving fourteen years. His wife throwing him a coming-home party in Teachwood. I think Cristal gon' be there too."

"When you talk to Cristal?" Hakim asked, still focusing on the road.

"I seen her at the mall earlier today."

"Shawty, how is she looking? I haven't seen that girl in years."

"She look even better than before."

Peaches stared at the back of Hakim's head with a jealous look on her face. "Hakim!" she yelled.

"What's up?"

"I am back here, you know."

He glanced at her through the rearview mirror. "Girl, we talking about one of our home-girls from the 'hood. Don't be looking like that."

Hakim had only known Peaches for two and a half hours, but she was already showing signs of envy. He'd picked her up at the Low-Low corner store, right before he'd gone in to buy a box of Black & Mild cigars. All the young drug dealers who hung out in front of the store sought to gain her interest, but she chose Hakim over all of them.

The drive to Money's house took thirty-five minutes. It was 9:55 p.m., and the clock was ticking. Hakim pulled into the question mark-shaped driveway of Money Mac's luxury mini-mansion, one he'd had custom built from the ground up. There was a black-on-back 500 Benz, a red Lexus LF sports car, a gray Aston Martin Rapide, and a gold Range Rover Sport, all parked on the front lawn.

"You can let me out right here. I'ma catch up with you at the party."

"I'll be there."

"You be easy, Peaches, and tell ya friend I'ma get at her," Todd replied as Peaches tossed him the box of pizza and he threw his Foot Locker bag over his shoulder.

"I'll let her know."

Todd climbed out of the car, and Peaches hopped in the front seat. As soon as Todd saw Hakim backing out of the driveway, he retrieved the spare key from the small birdhouse that hung above the gable and used it to go inside.

* * *

The inside of the mansion was richly decorated and furnished with beautiful money-green leather sofas. Even the marble floor had small images of $5 bills embedded in it. The fresh cent of sandalwood and frankincense filled the living room.

Todd set his Foot Locker shopping bag on the floor, right next to the fireplace. He walked into the expensive, luxury,

Italian-style kitchen and placed the box of pizza on the pearly-white counter. He felt good to be back home, even though it had been years since he'd stepped foot in his father's kitchen.

After eating a few slices of pizza, Todd noticed it was getting quite late, so he quickly jumped in the shower to freshen up a bit. When he got out, he went into the walk-in closet and grabbed his blue polo shirt, Akoo jeans, white Air Force 1 shoes, and blue Atlanta fitted cap. He quickly got dressed, grabbed the keys to the Benz off of the mantel, and strolled out the front door.

* * *

The parking lot was packed. Cars, along with members of the Bloods gang, and street hustlers blocked the front entrance of the apartment, drinking Grey Goose vodka and selling crack cocaine. Most of the customers who came through were businesspeople with good jobs, like school teachers, lawyers, and even a few doctors.

When Money's Benz pulled up, everyone cleared the front entrance to make way for Todd to drive through. Hakim and Chris spotted Money's car cruising slowly and instantly knew it was Todd, because Money wasn't expected back until the following week.

Hakim and Chris were dressed in black and green Army fatigues, as if they were getting ready for some kind of war. Hakim walked over to the corner of the street and waved at Todd, motioning him to park behind his car.

Todd pulled into the empty parking spot, then hopped out of the Benz like some don out of an Italian mob flick.

Gucci Mane's "Freaky Gurl" remix played over the

surround-sound speakers, and females from all over Atlanta danced, smoked laced, popped ecstasy pills, and drank alcoholic beverages straight out of the bottle.

Todd spotted Cristal standing there with Kee-Kee and Meyon, and they all had Hpnotiq in one hand and Absolut vodka in the other. Cristal looked really sexy in her cream-colored dress suit and her long ponytail hanging down her back. Todd's eyes stayed glued on her while she stood there talking and drinking with her friends.

Finally, Todd walked over to Hakim and Chris. "What y'all got going on over here?" he asked.

"Shit! Getting fucked up on these Heinekens," Hakim responded, his eyes bloodshot.

"What it do, big-timer?" Chris replied as he gave Todd some dap.

"Nothing much but this school shit!"

"Hakim told me someone stole your car. I already got my goons on the lookout, so if they find it, it'll be lights out for the fuck nigga."

Todd looked Chris up and down with a smile. He was happy to have two friends who were so loyal, like Grip and Mac-9 were to Money Mac.

"Brah, I haven't seen you in a minute!"

Chris looked around. "I know, right? What it been, like a year?"

"Somethin' like that. When yo' goons find my car, let me know who the nigga is first."

"Will do! Hey, I think I might be able to find my li'l sister too."

Todd was instantly excited, like a kid on his first roller-coaster ride. "Where she at, brah?"

"I don't know for sure just yet, but I been talking to some people who may be able to help me."

"If there's anything I can do, just let me know. How's your mother holding up?"

Chris dropped his head. "Still fucking with that dope. The only one who can help her now is God, because it's out of my hands."

Todd frowned and considered Chris's words. "Brah, I want you to know that it gets better. You and Hakim will always be my brothers from other mothers."

They all smiled at the same time.

Hakim and Chris started to explain to Todd how serious the street life was, and they told him how happy they were that he'd chosen to go down the right path.

"Here, brah. Fire this up," Chris said, reaching into his side pants pocket for an already rolled marijuana blunt.

Todd leaned over into the Benz for the lighter that sat in the ashtray, but a light tap on his back interrupted him, and he placed the blunt on the driver seat before he turned around to see who it was.

"Hey, Todd," a soft voice whispered.

He slowly turned toward the sweet-smelling fragrance, and Cristal leaned in and French kissed him directly in the mouth. Todd wanted her badly, and his dick was instantly hard, but the taste of vodka from her smooth lips alerted him that she was intoxicated and might not have been aware of what she was doing. He grabbed her by both shoulders and gently pushed her away. "Look, Cristal, I really do like you, but I refuse to take advantage of you."

Tears began to fill Cristal's eyes; it was the first time in her life when a man had been unwilling to take advantage of her. No one had ever rejected her advances before, drunk or otherwise.

Todd lightly wiped the tears from her eyes with his thumb. "Don't you start crying on me. You are my friend above anything. I was really happy to see you when I first pulled up. I mean, look at you—all beautiful and presentable in your dress suit," he said sincerely.

She began to blush. "Thank you, Todd. You're a real gentleman."

Todd smiled broadly, licking his bottom lip. "I try to be when I'm in the presence of a woman."

"I only came because you asked me to," she admitted.

Todd glanced over at Hakim and Kee-Kee, who were sitting on the hood of his Cutlass, french kissing. "I want you to know that I'm glad you came. Did you talk to Hakim and Chris yet?"

"Oh yes! They are still the same. Chris was talking about how you and him beat down Meco and his brother Rock."

Todd took a deep breath, as if he were irritated.

"What's wrong?" she asked with concern.

"Everything's good. Come here," he said, grabbing her by the waist.

They firmly embraced, and Cristal placed her head on Todd's chest, as if she were trying to listen to his heartbeat. He rested his chin on top of her head and closed his eyes.

"Say, pimp! Ain't your name Todd?" a deep, strong voice asked aggressively.

Todd raised his head quickly. MT stood at an arm's length away, with his fist balled up. He was biting on his bottom lip.

Todd's face formed into a frown, and he slightly shoved Cristal to the side. "Yeah, I'm Todd. What's up?" he asked.

MT took a step backward.

Cristal grabbed Todd by the forearm. "Come on, Todd."

Todd pulled away from her grip and pushed her slightly further away. "Cristal, stay out of this," he calmly said, keeping his eyes locked on MT.

"Let me holla at ya, my nigga."

"Okay. Let's walk," said Todd.

"Dig this, my nigga. That li'l ho you was talking to at the store—"

Todd cut him off right there. "Yeah? What about her, pimp?"

"That's my lady."

Todd started laughing. "My nigga, when I first seen you, I thought you was a player-ass nigga, but now I see you are a sucker-for-love-ass nigga who needs some serious help."

"I can be that, bitch-ass nigga—"

MT's words were immediately cut short by a straight left jab to his mouth. He leaned forward, and Todd caught him with an uppercut. Blood flowed from his nose as he struggled to regain his balance. When Todd saw the large crowd moving in to catch the action, he football tackled MT into the side of a gold Jaguar that was parked by the side of the road.

Hakim grabbed Todd from behind. "This me, brah. Calm down," he whispered in his friend's ear.

"Let me go, shawty! Fuck that pussy nigga."

Hakim released his grip. "Boy! If you ever come out yo' mouth sideways again, I'ma put you on your ass!" Todd yelled while trying to catch his breath.

MT slowly got to his feet with a smile on his face, blood dripping from his mouth, covering his Rocawear t-shirt.

Todd had to leave quickly, because his temper was getting overheated. One thing he wouldn't allow was someone disrespecting him or approaching him about a female. Todd hopped into the Benz, his temper flaring, and sped off.

* * *

The sun shone brightly as Money and Grip maneuvered through the busy New York traffic.

"How in God's name do people function this early in the morning?" Money complained to himself as he looked down at his watch. It was 8:15 a.m. and Grip was still stretched out in the back seat, taking a cat nap.

Money Mac arrived at the downtown Marriott, and as soon as he pulled into the parking lot, a gray-haired black valet walked up to his window. "Will you be staying here today, sir?" the valet asked respectfully.

"Yes I will. Can you watch my friend here while I run in and pay for the room?"

"I surely can, sir." He opened the door for Money to step out.

* * *

Money checked into Room 129, like always. When he got back to the car, Grip was standing next to the valet, smoking a cigarette.

I hope they got some good breakfast this time, because last time we were here, the food tasted like shit," said Grip.

"We can go grab a bite to eat up the road if you like."

Grip flicked the cigarette over into the crystal teardrop-shaped wishing well, causing the valet to look at him strangely. "Naw, we good, pimpin'. We got business to handle. Besides, it's about that time to let our associates know we're in town."

Katavious Ellis

Money waved the young Caucasian concierge to grab the brown Gucci suitcase, which contained $1 million in cash, and the valet hopped in the car to park it.

The concierge escorted Money and Grip to the elevator with their suitcase. Once they got to the seventh floor, Money tipped the young concierge with a $100 bill, and that made him very happy.

Inside the plush, fresh-smelling room, there were two neatly made king-sized beds against the wall, a stylish golden crystal chandelier hanging from the ceiling, and a medium-sized red oak nightstand next to the sliding glass doors that led out onto the patio, overlooking New York City.

Money Mac walked over to the nightstand and retrieved the cordless phone. "I've got to let them know we're in town," said Money, referring to his business associates.

Grip placed the suitcase on the bed, then removed his nickel-plated .45 caliber handgun from its holster. "Okay. I'm going in the bathroom to wash my face."

Money nodded his head while holding his phone to his ear.

"Hello?" a deep voice answered from the other end of the receiver.

"This me, Mr. Smith," Money replied using his code name. Money and his business associates always used code names over the phone, just in case the feds were tapping in on their calls.

"Mr. Smith, it's a pleasant surprise to hear from you on such short notice."

"Yes, I made it in ahead of schedule. Being late is bad business, but being early means business is more important than not being here at all."

The man started laughing through the receiver. "Okay. Very well then. When the stars fill the sky and the streets become untroubled, we meet," he stated in code.

Money knew he was talking about meeting at the warehouse around 10 o'clock that night. "I'll be there," he confirmed.

"I hope you like it here."

"Oh, I will."

Money Mac hung up the phone, then walked over to the bed and lay down. While staring at the ceiling, he quickly dozed off with his mouth wide open.

* * *

Hours later, Money woke up feeling rejuvenated.

Grip sat up at the table eating lobster, shrimp, and oven-baked breadsticks. "I ordered room service. You want any?" Grip asked when he saw Money sitting up with his back against the headboard.

Money rotated his neck clockwise, then stretched his arms above him.

"We got to get going, so get yourself together pimpin' and hit GG and Jay-Bo to let em know we pulling out," said Money.

"Okay. I'm finished with this anyway. You might wanna try these buttery breadsticks. I think they have a black woman making these, because they are good as a mother-fucker."

Money unzipped the suitcase. Two twin .40 Glocks and four fully loaded clips lay between the stacks of money. He unfastened the straps on his gun holster and placed the pistols in it.

* * *

The night was silent, and the moon was full. Cars pulled in and out of the Marriott hotel parking lot. Money and Grip stood at the curb, waiting for the valet to bring the car around. Money looked down at his watch and saw that it was 8:45 p.m.

Seconds later, the valet pulled up right in front of them. "Sorry it took me a while, sir."

"It's no problem," Money stated. He placed the suitcase in the back seat of his SS Monte Carlo, then popped the trunk for Grip.

Grip grabbed a large black bag from the trunk. He hopped into the passenger seat and unzipped the bag. Inside it was an M-16 with three banana clasps.

"Just be on point and watch my back," Money replied, wearing a serious look.

Grip cocked a bullet into the chamber. "You already know I got your back, pimpin'."

At 9:55 p.m., Money drove into the run-down warehouse that was surrounded by barbed wire fence. Grip surveyed the area very closely as a Lincoln limousine pulled into the front entrance. GG and Jay-Bo pulled up minutes later and parked on the backside of the warehouse.

Money Mac parked right behind the limo. "Show time," he said as he and Grip stepped out of the car in their tailor-made, pinstriped suits. Grip was fully armed with the M-16 machinegun.

Two Italian men dressed in black business suits stood in front of the limo, armed with AK-47 rifles. Next, the back door of the limo flew open, and two heavyset, Caucasian men, also in business suits, stepped out.

Grip scanned the perimeter carefully with his eyes, while Money observed the men with the guns.

"Gentlemen, it's so nice to have you all with us tonight. This here is Mr. Kenneth, and I'm Jacob. Unfortunately, Mr. Devon couldn't make it, so—"

Money Mac threw his hand up, signifying that Jacob should stop talking. "Hold up! What you mean Mr. Devon 'couldn't make it'? I only do business with the boss man himself."

Jacob grabbed his noticeable gun. "Mr. Smith, he had a very important meeting to attend."

Money smiled angrily. "If his meeting is more important than this, I don't need to be here either. Come on, Grip. Let's go!" Money then turned to walk off, while Grip kept his eyes locked on the two gunmen.

"Mr. Smith, wait a minute!"

Money stopped walking. "I'm listening," he said.

"Let me call Mr. Devon's personal cell for you."

"Yeah, you do that."

Jacob reached in his inside coat pocket very slowly and pulled out a small cell phone. Money and Grip stood side by side, ready for whatever might come their way. It was the first time Mr. Devon had not shown up in person to handle their business transaction, so Money couldn't help begin suspicious.

"Mr. Smith, the boss wants to speak with you," said Jacob.

"Stay on point," Money whispered to Grip. He then approached Jacob boldly, staring into his eyes as if he were trying to read his every thought. When Jacob held the phone out for him to take, Money glanced down at his hand and saw that he was trembling. "You okay?" Money asked, just to see what his response would be.

Jacob did just as Money thought he would do: He nodded his head, then looked at the ground.

Money gave off a slight grin as he held the phone to his ear. "Hello?"

"Yes? I am here. Mr. Jacob tells me you're not pleased with doing business with him."

"I don't even know these guys. For all I know, they could be undercover feds."

Jacob quickly shifted his head toward money.

"I can assure you, they are not feds. I had to send my two trustworthy men. This meeting is very important."

"I only do business with you—not some middlemen."

"Calm down, Mr. Smith. I'll tell you what. Do business with Jacob and Kenneth, and I'll give you a couple extra kilos."

Money thought for a moment. Mr. Devon had never spoken of kilos over the phone; only in person did any of them ever dare mention anything about drugs. It was all the evidence he needed that something was up, and Money was willing to give him the rope to hang himself. "Okay. This one time, I'll conduct business without you being present—but ONLY this time."

"I fully understand, Mr. Smith."

"Let's hope so," Money said, then tossed the phone back to Jacob, who barely caught it with both hands. "Now, let's get down to business, gentlemen," Money said, walking back toward Grip. When he got close enough for Grip to hear, he whispered, "Devon want us out the picture," and he and Grip made their way to the back of the car to grab the suitcase with the cash.

"Yeah, I felt like that the minute I laid eyes on them. So… what we doing?"

Money took off his suit jacket and laid it across the back seat of his car. He then checked the chamber of his Glock to make sure a bullet was in position to fire. "Simple. We take these fools out the picture first. We kill them and take everything."

Grip simply nodded as he saw Jay-Bo and GG peering through the building stained glass window.

* * *

Inside the warehouse, it was very quiet. Three heavily dusty heat lights hung above a large metal table, where all the business transactions took place.

Money stood on one side of the table, with Grip behind him, ready for whatever. Jacob, Kenneth, and the two gunmen stood on the opposite side of the table.

"So, where's the money, Mr. Smith?" Jacob smoothly asked.

Money put the suitcase down with his right hand. "Oh, it's right here, but you first. This is how Mr. Devon and I conduct business."

Jacob snapped his fingers, and the gunman on the right of him walked into a small room and came out with a duffel bag filled with sixty-five kilos, all neatly wrapped in plastic.

Money whipped out his blade and cut into one of the packages. "This is some kind of that straight-off-the-ship, pure Peruvian flake," he stated while tasting a sample. When Money reached down for the suitcase, he felt the cold of stainless steel pressed against his temple.

Money didn't know that Grip was stretched out on the

floor like a doormat with blood spurting from the back of his head. The unknown gunman had crept down from the ceiling like Special Forces and had hit Grip hard with the butt of the gun.

Money looked over at Jacob and Kenneth with an evil eye. "So this is Devon's way of showing me his welcome?"

The other two gunmen stood guard while Jacob grabbed the suitcase from the floor and Kenneth grabbed the duffel bag off the table.

The unknown gunman removed Money's two Glocks from his holster, then tossed them on the floor.

"It's nothing personal, Mr. Smith—only business, if you know what I mean," Jacob proudly said with a smile.

The gunman pushed Money to his knees, pointing a .357 revolver to his head.

Money looked back and saw Grip lying there out cold, his face surrounded by blood. "I know what you mean, Mr. Jacob."

"Yes, Mr. Smith?"

"You will die."

Jacob grinned. "You're in no position to be making threats."

Just as the gunman raised his pistol to shoot Money, Jay-Bo and GG came running through the front door, firing multiple rounds with M-16 machineguns. Kenneth and the two bodyguards fell to the pavement like chopped wood as bullets flew, violently penetrating their flesh.

Jacob dropped the suitcase and ran toward the exit door.

When Money saw that the gunman had taken his eyes off of him for a split second, he reached out quickly and snatched the pistol out of his hand and shot the gunman twice in the kneecap.

He fell to the ground, clutching at his knee with both hands, blood gushing through his fingers as he screamed for dear God.

Money stood to his feet and emptied three rounds of hollow-point bullets into the gunman, then looked over at Jay-Bo and GG with a killer's expression on his face. "You two grab the money and the kilos," he demanded.

Grip began to regain consciousness and struggled to get to his feet. "Ah! Fuck! My head hurt," he said, groaning and holding his head.

"Get him out of here!"

GG placed the duffel bag over his shoulder, then helped Grip to his feet.

"Say, Money, what are you going to do?" Jay-Bo asked.

Money grabbed his twin Glocks from the concrete floor. "I got to go get that fool Jacob. He ain't gone far."

"Okay. We'll be waiting for you in the parking lot. Be careful."

Money crept through the dark, creepy hallways of the warehouse with caution. He could smell the scent of Jacob's cheap cologne hovering in the air. The sound of shattering glass echoed from a back room that led to the parking lot. Money quickly sped up his pace, keeping his pistols positioned for open fire. A dark shadow zoomed past the window, and Money let off a few rounds from each gun.

"Ah!" a deep, raspy voice shouted from outside.

Money peeked around the corner from the exit door and saw Jacob crawling through a puddle of his own blood. Two of the bullets from Money's .40 Glocks had penetrated Jacob's shoulder and back. An evil smile appeared on Money's face. He slowly walked over to Jacob's paralyzed body. "I told you

I was going to kill you, you fat fuck! Now look at you—all fucked up and shit."

Jacob held his arm out, and blood dripped from his fingertips. "I was only following orders from Mr. Devon. Please don't kill me."

GG and Grip came speeding through the parking lot in Money's SS Monte Carlo like madmen, and Jay-Bo was trailing behind them in his grayish-black Mercedes-Benz ML6.

"So, tell me, you fat fuck, where's Devon at right now?" Money demanded, standing over Jacob with both pistols pointed squarely at his head.

Jacob began coughing up blood. He struggled to get his words out. "He's…he's at the Moonlight Special over on 24th in Brooklyn."

Money stared into his eyes as if he was trying to reach his soul. "You don't deserve to live another minute, you disloyal coward."

The sound of police sirens continuously resonated from a distance.

Jay-Bo reached over to the passenger door and pushed it open. "Let's roll, baby. The cops is coming, and I damn sho ain't trying to get lockdown in New York!"

Money slowly raised both pistols and emptied both clips, until smoke came from the barrels. Jacob's body jerked then his eyes rolled to the back of his head while Money stood over him, waiting until his last breath. "Now we can go," Money said, looking at Jay-Bo.

SCHOOL BOY

* * *

Meanwhile, after Todd left the party, he decide to stop by Clark Atlanta College to grab a few items from his room. His blue polo shirt and knuckles were stained with small spots of blood, from when he'd punched MT in the mouth. When Todd pulled into the circle-shaped parking lot, he parked next to the handicap parking spot and fired up the already rolled marijuana blunt Chris had passed to him before MT disrupted his day. He inhaled the smoke slowly, hoping it would calm his nerves a bit.

I shoulda stayed on that nigga's ass for real, he thought while he rested his head on the headrest.

A group of teen college students was sitting on a wooden bench under a large pine tree, having some kind of gathering.

Todd got out of the car and headed for his room. When he got there, the door was unlocked, so he peeked in first, before walking in.

The lights were dimmed, and slow music was playing on the small boom-box that sat next to the window that overlooked the parking lot. Richard and a beautiful redheaded white girl with tattoos all over her arms were on his bed, cuddling.

"Come in, roomie. It's just me and my friend April lying in here cooling," said Richard.

Todd stepped into the room, his eyes blazing red from the marijuana blunt. "I'll only be a few seconds."

"You good. This is your room as well as mine."

Todd nodded his head and flicked on the light switch. *Damn! That li'l white ho is fine!* he thought when April turned over on her stomach to show off her pink Mojo boy shorts.

Richard looked over at Todd and winked.

Todd smiled, then walked into the small closet. He grabbed the Nike shoebox from the top shelf—the one with black tape wrapped around it. Inside the box was a chrome .380 handgun, along with two clips and a box of bullets. Right before he had graduated from high school, his father had encouraged him to buy a gun in case he might ever need it because killings in the streets of Atlanta were at an all-time high.

After gathering the items out of the box, Todd placed them in his brown leather backpack and strolled out the door. He wasn't about to let MT catch him slipping without a piece.

* * *

The students who'd been sitting under the tree when he'd first parked were gone, and the parking lot was empty.

Todd hopped in the Benz and reclined in the driver seat, with thoughts of Beautiful on his mind. He stared up at the dark sky, contemplating whether or not he should call her. "Fuck it. Why not?" he mumbled, grabbing his cell phone from the compartment.

There were five missed calls from Hakim. Todd deleted them, then dialed Beautiful's number, which was already programmed into his phone.

"Hello?" she answered in a sleepy voice.

The feeling of excitement overwhelmed Todd when she picked up. "What's good, Beautiful?" he replied, doing his best Barry White impression.

Beautiful instantly knew it was Todd, but she decided to play a mind game with him. "Who's this?" she said with a smile.

"This Todd."

"Sorry, but I don't know a Todd."

Todd looked puzzled. "Damn, shawty! It's like that?"

"Look, I don't know you, so get off my line," she snapped, then hung up. Beautiful lay back on her bed, smiling.

Todd tossed his phone on the passenger seat. There was a crazy, confused look on his face. "That bitch needs help. She got to be suffering from a case of amnesia." A second later, his iPhone began ringing. He glanced over at the screen and saw that it was Beautiful calling back. "Oh shit! That crazy bitch," he said to himself before answering.

"Hey, Todd," she said, grinning.

"Oh, so now you know who I am?"

"Yes," she replied in a childish voice.

"What are you getting into this time of night?"

"To be honest with you, I'm just lying in bed. I didn't think you would call after finding out old boy jumped on me today 'cause I know the whole school talking bout it."

"What? Come on, baby girl. Real men don't turn their backs on a woman in her time of need. Hell, if I had been there, I'da stood up for you."

Beautiful began to blush. "Aw! You made me smile."

"That's what's up. Now, make me smile by coming outside so I can see that pretty face."

There was no response from Beautiful.

"Hello? You still there?"

She cleared her throat. "Yes, I'm here. You want me to come outside right now?"

"No...tomorrow. Yeah, now!" he joked.

"Boy, anyway, I just got out of the shower. Why don't you

just come to my room? I'm on the first floor."

"You know if I get caught—"

She cut in and said, "Don't worry. You won't get caught. You coming or what?"

"Okay. I'm coming now. When I get to the front door, I'ma call you so you can buzz me in."

"All right, baby boy."

* * *

As soon as Beautiful hung up with Todd, she immediately started cleaning her room so Todd wouldn't think she lived like a pig. Clothes were everywhere on the floor, along with shoes, and there were dishes all around the place; a glass, cereal bowl, and plastic spoon were right at the head of the twin-sized bed. Once she saw that everything was neatly in order, she walked into the bathroom and put on some of her cherry lip gloss and black eyeliner. She started to hide all the teddy bears MT had bought for her, but a sudden knock at the door startled her.

She stood behind the door with a terrified look on her face. She had been expecting Todd to call so she could buzz him in. *Damn! I hope this isn't MT*, she thought.

The knocking continued.

"Beautiful? It's me, Todd!" the voice yelled from the other side of the door.

Beautiful felt a sudden relief when she heard Todd's voice and quickly unlocked the door. She stood before Todd in her silk green nightgown, and his eyes locked on her like a heat-seeking missile. She grabbed him by the hand. "Come on in, boy. How did you get in without me buzzing you though?"

Todd smiled, observing how neat her room was. "Some girl was going out the door, so I waited until she turned her back and crept in."

"I gotta watch you."

"Why you say that?"

She placed her hand on her hip. "You creeping past people like James Bond and shit."

They both laughed.

"I see you got jokes tonight. Who's your roommate?"

"My friend Peaches. Why?"

"I was just asking, because y'all living clean up in here." Todd walked over to the bed with all the stuffed animals on top.

"Yes, that's my bed," she quickly replied.

He grabbed one of the teddy bears, then sat on the edge of the bed. "You scared to sleep alone or something?"

"Naw, boy. I had most of them since I was a child," she lied, speaking the first thing that came to mind.

Todd reclined on his elbows. He noticed the bruise above Beautiful's cheek, but he paid no mind to that flaw, because his lustful eyes were caught on the dark green thong that fit her firm ass perfectly under the sheer night gown. "I heard your old boy jumped on you today."

She lowered her head, as if she were ashamed.

Todd got up from the bed and walked over to Beautiful. "Lift your head up, baby girl. You are in good hands now. No nigga will hit you again as long as I'm living." He gently clutched her chin.

Beautiful slowly lifted her head, and Todd leaned in to kiss her lips. "Why do you have blood on your shirt?" she asked, shifting her head to prevent his kiss. She wanted to kiss him as much as he wanted to kiss her, but giving herself to him that quick just wasn't going to happen. Beautiful had vowed that she would never have sex with another man until she first found out what his intentions were with her.

"I had to beat your boy's ass tonight at the party."

Beautiful's eyes grew wide, and her mouth hung open. "Who? MT?"

Todd strolled around the room. "Yeah. He walked up on me talking about you his girl and some mo' ho shit, so I punched him in the mouth a few times."

Beautiful couldn't believe what she was hearing. The thought of MT getting beaten down brought joy into her life. She was so excited that she grabbed Todd by the back of his neck and kissed him right on the mouth.

Todd was surprised to see Beautiful so happy.

"Did you get him good?" she asked.

"Damn right!"

"Boy, you too pretty to be fighting."

A grave expression came over Todd's face. "Pretty? Shawty, I'm handsome. Fuck niggas who think they're pretty," he replied, looking her directly in the eyes.

"Oh my God! Don't take it the wrong way. All I'm saying is that you don't look like the type who'd be fighting."

Todd smirked. "I know. Them niggas be thinking that too, until I get on their asses like Ali. Don't get me wrong...I don't like fighting, but if someone push me, I'ma handle mine."

Beautiful stared at Todd's lips like she wanted to taste them once more.

"What color are your eyes?"

"Blue!" he joked.

She tapped him gently on the shoulder. "Boy, stop playing!

Your eyes ain't blue."

"Naw, for real. They're green."

"I ain't never seen a brown-skinned nigga with green eyes."

"You see one now. Where are your rings you had on earlier?" he asked, grabbing her hand.

She glanced down at her hand before speaking. "That stupid-ass nigga took 'em."

"That ain't no way to treat a woman. Niggas nowadays just don't understand what it takes to keep a woman."

Beautiful smiled, and her eyes twinkled like stars.

"What?" Todd asked.

"Nothing. I just love the way you're talking."

Todd slowly leaned toward Beautiful, until their lips locked. Beautiful showed no signs of resistance this time. In fact, she loved every moment of Todd's gentle hands touching her body. He carefully laid her back on the bed, kissing her around the neck, and his manhood began to get noticeably hard.

"No, Todd."

"What's wrong?"

"I'm not ready for this yet. I need you to just hold me tight."

Todd rolled off of her and stood to his feet. "If you're not ready, I can wait."

Beautiful stood as well and stepped closer to Todd. "I don't want you to be mad at me. It's just—"

He placed his index finger over her lips. "Baby girl, I am not mad because you won't have sex with me. I want to love you, not misuse you."

A tear fell from her eye, and Todd embraced her with a

firm hug. He knew that after what MT had put her through, she needed comfort and love.

They stayed up talking for hours. Todd looked at his watch and saw that it was 2:00 on the dot. He kissed Beautiful on her forehead, then got up off the bed. "It's getting late, baby girl. I gotta get going."

"Okay. Let me walk you to the door," she said, half-asleep.

Todd turned toward her when they got to the hallway. "I will not hurt you."

She gave him a slight smile. "I believe in you, Todd."

"That's what's up. Can I give you some before I leave."

"Sure, baby."

He wrapped his arms around her waist and pulled her closer to him. Before she could say a word, he french kissed her.

Beautiful wrapped her arms around his neck while standing on the tips of her toes. She felt Todd's manhood swelling against her stomach, so she pulled away with a smile. "Thank you for that," she replied, looking down at his dick print.

Todd, embarrassed, simply said, "Goodnight," and walked off.

* * *

Beautiful closed her bedroom door, walked over to the bed, and fell backward, still blushing.

Minutes later, Peaches came storming through the front door, her eyes bloodshot from marijuana smoke. "Girl, you won't believe what happened at the party tonight!" she started, stripping down to her panties.

"I already heard."

Peaches quickly snapped her head in Beautiful's direction. "So that was Todd I just saw jumping over the fence when I was coming in?"

"Yup."

"Look at you over there smiling with your nasty ass!"

"Bitch, please! We didn't do shit but hold each other and talk."

"But anyway, that nigga know he fine, girl."

"Yeah. He's my boo, and MT's lame ass is out of my life for good."

* * *

The Marriott hotel was buzzing with activity. Hundreds of men and women were gathered in the parking lot, waiting on the shuttle buses to take them over to the Apollo Theater, where the B.E.T. Awards were being held.

Jay-Bo and Money Mac saw that the hotel parking lot was too packed, so they pulled into T.G.I. Friday's, with GG and Grip following behind them.

GG pulled up to the passenger door, where Money was sitting. "So, what do we do from here?" he asked, leaning his head out the window and holding a cigarette between his fingers.

Money glanced at his watch. It was 12:00 a.m., and his adrenaline was rushing at a tremendous rate. The only thing playing through his mind was murder, and he was willing to do whatever it took to finish what had been started. He looked over at Jay-Bo, who was sitting calmly in the driver seat, with his left hand gripping the steering wheel, and then he glanced back at GG. "Before we head back to Atlanta, we first pay Devon a visit."

"I'm up for that," GG and Jay-Bo said at the same time.

"Say, Grip, you all right over there, pimpin'?"

Grip was lying in the passenger seat of Money's SS Monte Carlo, with a shirt held against the back of his bloody head. "You already know I'm good, pimpin'. I can't let Devon live after how he tried us," he said, trying to deal with the pain from the gash in his head.

Money wore an evil grin. "Let's go to the Moonlight Special over on 24th in Brooklyn."

Without a word, Jay-Bo sped out of the parking lot.

* * *

It was 1:45 a.m. when Jay-Bo, Money, GG, and Grip arrived at the Moonlight Special in Brooklyn. The club was considered the raunchiest in New York, but it was among the most profitable, thanks to Jim Jones. He and rapper Jadakiss performed there regularly for standing-room-only crowds. Devon paid them both thousands of dollars a week in cash to keep his club up and running.

The line outside Moonlight Special stretched two blocks down Bookly Street. The crowd was so unruly that the security guards had to set up barricades to keep the overanxious women from cutting in line. Friday nights had become chaotic since Jim Jones and Jadakiss performed on those evenings.

Jay-Bo parked on the corner, right across from Moonlight Special. GG pulled up behind him.

Money Mac spotted Devon's black Bentley limousine parked in front of the walkway that led to the VIP rooms. He stared down the dark alley that led to the Moonlight fire exit, then glanced over at the two muscular, well-built security guards who were directing traffic in the parking lot. "Park in between them two cars," said Money.

Jay-Bo parallel-parked the SS Monte Carlo between a green Jeep Grand Cherokee RT8 and a red Chrysler 300. GG pulled up alongside him and lowered the window.

"Y'all park in the alley, in case Devon tries to escape down the fire exit. Me and Jay-Bo going inside to make our presence known," Money said, still wearing a devilish grin on his face.

GG made a U-turn in the middle of the street, turned off the headlights, and pulled into the alley.

Grip placed a bullet in the chamber of his M-16 machinegun. "I'm killing any mother-fucker that come down that fire exit."

GG kissed the side of his .40 Glock. "This bitch here has never failed me because I treat her with love."

Grip smirked, then fired up a cigarette. "Let's stay on point, young blood."

"Always," GG calmly responded, staring down the gloomy alley, through the rearview mirror.

Money Mac and Jay-Bo walked around to the trunk of Jay-Bo's Mercedes-Benz and pulled out two bulletproof vests, a black leather trench coat, and an AK-47 machinegun. They both put on vests, and Jay-Bo grabbed the trench coat and AK-47, while Money checked the chamber of his twin .40 Glocks in his holster.

After making sure everything was cocked and loaded, Money Mac and Jay-Bo strolled over to the three security guards who stood at the front entrance of the Moonlight Special.

"Follow my lead," Money replied, gripping the handle of his twin Glocks.

Jay-Bo cuffed the AK-47 inside the trench coat as they crossed the busy street. "I got your back, pimpin'."

Money smiled.

All three security guards were busy trying to keep the crowd in order, so Money and Jay-Bo slid right past them without having to use any force to gain entry.

"Sir, that will be $100 for the both of you," the young, Italian-looking hostess yelled from behind the cashier's booth.

Jay-Bo and Money Mac quickly turned around, and the young hostess's eyes grew big when she saw the guns hanging from Money's holster. "You want $100, bitch? I got you right here!" Money Mac angrily stated as he drew his gun and fired two rounds into the glass.

The hostess stood behind the glass, holding her chest. When she opened her eyes, she realized she'd not been hit by the hot slugs. The two slugs had barely penetrated the bulletproof glass, but that didn't stop the club cashier from being overwhelmed with fear and shock, causing her to panic and fall into a fetal position on the floor.

As the loud music blared through the club, the shots went virtually unheard.

Money Mac laughed to himself. "You are one lucky bitch."

Jay-Bo looked out the front door to make sure the security guards didn't hear the gunshots.

"Come on, Jay-Bo. Let's give this Devon character a real fucking performance."

Jay-Bo smiled. "Yeah! He fucked with the wrong city

niggas."

"It's time to show this mother-fucker what Hotlanta stand for," Money replied, wiping the sweat from his forehead.

* * *

Two white Chevrolet Sport trucks with dark-tinted windows pulled up in front of the Moonlight Special nightclub. Three men got out of each truck, dressed in all black, as if they were members of the Special Forces, fully armed with P-90 machineguns.

"What the fuck?" GG shouted when he saw the six men approaching the club; the security guards demanded that the crowd stand back and let them through.

Grip immediately rose up in the passenger seat. "What's going on?" he asked.

"Let's get moving. Them six commando-looking mother-fuckers is going into the club, and they're packing hot heat."

Without wasting time to answer, Grip climbed out of the car with his M-16 and started making his way toward the armed men.

GG followed behind him, tightly gripping his Glock in one hand and a nickel-plated submachine gun in the other.

Just as the gunmen were about to enter the glass double doors of the club, Grip called out to them, "Yo, fellas!"

Before they could turn around, Grip and GG opened fire. The few people who were still in line scattered like a group of ants. Bullets tore through the commandos' flesh rapidly, before they ever knew what hit them.

The three security guards let off a few rounds, but Grip and GG took cover behind a pink Infiniti that was parked on the side of the street. Four of the gunmen laid down on the pavement, while the other two laid in a puddle of their own blood, deeply wounded.

Grip peeked through the window of the Infiniti to see what the security guard was doing. He saw them slowly creeping toward them like trained assassins.

GG sat on the ground with his back against the tire, breathing heavily. "So? What do we do now?" he asked, looking at Grip.

"Shit! We kill these dog-ass mother-fuckers before they kill us. I'll tell you what. We gotta move fast, because they're coming. Come here for a second."

GG carefully stood to his feet, keeping his back bent. "What's up?"

"Do you see that blue van parked on the corner right there?" Grip asked, motioning to the corner that led to the circular parking lot.

"Yeah, I see it," he responded, removing his long dreadlocks from over his eyes.

"Since you're younger and more athletic than me, take off and run toward the van. When their attention is drawn to you, I'll drop them like a bad habit."

GG smiled. "I can do that. Here. Take this submachine gun. I can run faster with just this Glock."

Grip leaned over the trunk of the car with both guns aimed directly at the security guards. "I'm ready when you are," he said to GG.

GG looked down at his smoke-gray Air Force shoes to make sure the laces were tied tight. "Let's do this. I'm ready."

"I'm already in position, so do what you do."

GG was about five-nine, with the physique of Wesley

Snipes and the looks of a dreadlocked Denzel Washington. He took off running like a bat out of hell and then fired a few rounds at the security guards.

The guards immediately reacted by returning shots. Bullets flew past GG's head as he ran in a zigzag angle.

Without delay, Grip let off multiple rounds of gunfire from the automatic weapons. The streaming hot flying cop-killer bullets swept the guards off their feet.

"Now that's how we do it in the A, you mother-fuckers!" Grip yelled after seeing that his plan was a success.

GG leaned against the van, holding his chest with his left hand as he tried to catch his breath. "Man, I gotta stop smoking weed," he mumbled to himself.

Grip waved GG over. "Come on! We got some unfinished business to handle."

* * *

The large disco lights hanging from the ceiling rotated in a circle, sending reflections of various colors around the room. Jim Jones performance had the crowd crunk, and smoke from cigarettes filled the atmosphere, with all types of fragrances blending in with it.

Money and Jay-Bo boldly stood next to the triangular glass counter bar like they owned the place.

The bartender was serving a young white lady, who looked to be in her early twenties. He put a glass of liquor down in front of her, then noticed the two guns hanging from Money's holster. "May I help you, Officer?" the plus-sized, gray-headed Italian bartender asked. He took Money for a cop, due to how neatly dressed he was and the fact that security would not have let anyone inside with a gun unless he was with the police.

Money Mac played along. "Yes, you can help me, sir."

The bartender wiped his hands with a white towel he had hanging over his shoulder. "What can I assist you with? Been a busy night in here."

"Well, I'm looking for Mr. Devon. I have a few questions to ask him before—"

The bartender cut him off. "Mr. Devon is busy at the moment. Leave a card or something, and I'll make sure he gets it."

Money had to think of something fast, because the bartender was playing hardball. "Look…come a li'l closer so I can tell you something."

The bartender leaned over the counter to hear what Money had to say.

"I'm not supposed to be telling you this because I could get fired, but the big dogs down at City Hall will be coming to shut Mr. Devon down and put him away for life. Now, I am his only hope, so I suggest you tell me where he's at."

Jay-Bo stood by the dance floor, looking around, with his AK-47 cuffed inside his long black trench coat.

The bartender stepped back from the counter with a surprised look on his face. "He's in that back room right next to them two drink machines."

Money reached his hand over the counter and gave him a handshake. "Thank you for your cooperation," he replied with a straight face.

The bartender went back to serving drinks.

Money Mac and Jay-Bo strolled to the back of the club, trying not to draw any attention to what was about to take place. Once they got to the door, Jay-Bo tossed the trench coat on the floor, and Money pulled out his two Glock .40s.

"Kick the door in! It's locked," Money said, jiggling the doorknob. Jay-Bo stood six-one and had the shoe size of Shaquille O'Neal, so Money was sure he'd have no problem with the door.

The sweat from Jay-Bo's dreadlocks rolled down the center of his back. He was a little nervous, wondering what might be waiting for them when they entered the room. Meh, any real killer would be nervous, he thought. "The hell with it! I came for this shit," he said with great confidence. He raised his right foot to a level he was comfortable with, then kicked right above the lock as hard as he could; the door flew right open.

Money Mac rushed into the plush, luxury conference room with both pistols drawn on the arrogant Italian mobster, who was sitting at a large circular table, conducting a meeting. All the men remained in their seats, with surprised looks on their faces. Devon, on the other hand, was reclined in his seat, wearing a grin that said he wasn't afraid. Money knew the men had to be some type of mob bosses because of the tailor-made suits they wore. But hell, he didn't care. His beef wasn't with them. All he wanted was Devon.

Jay-Bo quickly closed the door, placed his back against the wall, and aimed the AK-47 directly at Devon.

"Oh, so you think this here's a game, Mr. Devon?" Money angrily said.

Devon placed both of his hands on top of the table. "Do you really think you can come into my club, waving your gun around like some fucking madman, and get away with it? You disrespect me in front of my fellow men, you fucking foolish monkey."

Money walked over to Devon and smacked him in the mouth with the barrel of the gun. Devon's head jerked backward, and he immediately covered his mouth with both hands. Blood permeated through his fingers like a water stream.

Money Mac aggressively grabbed him by the back of his shirt collar. "Get your fat ass up! Gentlemen, please do not take this personally. I want nothing from you all. Mr. Devon here thought he could just take my hard-earned money and kill me."

"So…can we leave?" the tall, pecan-colored mobster with the neatly trimmed, grayish goatee fearfully asked.

"Yeah, but first let me handle my unfinished business with my friend here, Mr. Devon." Money held one gun to Devon's temple and one to his throat. "I'll tell you what, Devon. If you can get me $1 million in cash right now, I won't let my friend over there shoot you dead. Now, do we have a deal?"

Mr. Devon nodded his head, then tapped on the table. All three grabbed their briefcases from the floor, and Jay-Bo quickly aimed the chopper at them.

"Don't shoot, young man. Mr. Devon wants us to hand this money over to you," the heavyset, tan-skinned mobster who looked to be in his late forties said.

"We don't want you all's money. We want Devon's money for doing bad business with us," Money said smoothly.

"This is Mr. Devon's money. We are only here to pay him the money we're being extorted for."

Money looked down at Devon, who was now leaning over the table, wiping his bloody mouth with his necktie. "You son of a bitch! First, you set me up to get killed, and now you're abusing your authority by extorting people? You are full of surprises, Devon—and not the fucking good kind."

The heavyset mobster unlocked his briefcase, then slid it across the table to Money. "Here. That briefcase has $400,000 in it, and there's $300,000 in each of the other two."

Money Mac put one of his pistols back in the holster, then closed the briefcase. "Sit your ass back down, you fat fuck!" Money demanded, pushing Devon back into his chair. "Jay-Bo, grab the other two briefcases so we can get out of here. Mr. Devon, I am a man of my word, so tonight, you'll live. Let's go, Jay-Bo."

Jay-Bo exited the room with the AX-47 strapped to his shoulder and two of the briefcases in hand.

Devon sat back in his chair and took a deep breath when he saw Money getting ready to exit through the door.

"Oh, Mr. Devon...I almost forgot," Money said. He turned around and shot Devon right in the center of his forehead.

The back of Devon's head burst open in halos of blood, and brain matter covered the back wall.

Money then looked over at the three men. "Thank you, gentlemen, for your time. Bonne nuit," Money replied in French, telling them, "Goodnight."

"Bien venu," the heavyset mobster said, meaning, "You're welcome."

Money Mac then he smiled and walked out the door.

* * *

The crowd was still jumping up and down, waving red and blue neon light sticks in their hands. The lights were slightly dimmed in the place, and Jim Jones was performing on the large stage at the center of the club.

Money Mac followed behind Jay-Bo, focusing on the bartender as he reached behind the counter for a double-barreled shotgun.

When the bartender raised his shotgun to shoot Jay-Bo in the back, Money let off five rounds. The bullets hit empty rocks glasses, giving the bartender enough time to take cover behind the counter.

"Fuck! How in the hell I miss that mother-fucker?" Money angrily said with both guns still pointed at the bar.

The sound from Money's gun echoed over the loud performance, and the thick crowd started running toward the exit door like a bull stampede, people tripping and walking over each other like they were doormats to be stepped on.

Jay-Bo immediately turned around and saw GG and Grip boldly strolling through the double doors with their weapons aimed and ready to fire.

Jay-Bo looked over at Money Mac. "What happened?" he asked.

The bartender was going to shoot you in your back," said Money, with his pistols still aimed at the bar.

"We got to get moving!" Grip stated in a deep tone of voice.

Money and Jay-Bo glanced over at Grip and GG at the same time.

The bartender slowly raised himself up from behind the counter. Shards of broken glass fell from his shoulder, and his knees cracked as he stood, his old age overtaking him.

"Watch yourself, Money!" GG yelled, waving his submachine gun toward the bartender.

"No! No! No! Don't shoot! I'm unarmed," the bartender said, raising both hands in the air.

With his hands wrapped tightly around both pistols, Money turned his attention back to the terrified bartender. The look on Money's face indicated that he wasn't willing to let the old bartender live.

Four words flashed through the bartender's mind as he watched GG, Grip, Money, and Jay-Bo form a line and aim their weapons directly at him: Go for your gun. The plus-sized, Italian, gray-haired bartender felt as if he was going to die anyway, so he followed through with it and went for the double-barreled shotgun that was lying on the floor behind the counter.

The room lit up like the Fourth of July, and a spray of bullets entered the bartender's flesh from all angles, ripping through his body tissue like a chainsaw.

CHAPTER 6

Todd reached over on the nightstand and knocked the buzzing alarm clock onto the hardwood floor of Money's guest room. He rolled over on his stomach and buried his face in the pillow, trying to hide his eyes from the sunlight that was shining through the silky white curtains.

When Todd realized he couldn't go back to sleep, he slowly sat up in bed. He looked at Cristal, who was lying next to him, sound asleep like a newborn baby. He stared at her face for a moment, admiring her smooth, honey-brown skin, then reached his hand toward her and gently grabbed her shoulder.

Cristal slowly opened her eyes, and a peaceful smile came over her face. Her lips parted as she scratched the surface of her forearm. "What time is it?" she said, looking up at Todd.

He gently ran his fingers through her jet-black hair. "It's 8 o'clock."

"Oh, okay. It's still early then."

"How did you sleep last night?"

She gave him a small smile. "I slept pretty good, thanks to you."

After Todd had left Beautiful's room the night before, he'd driven to Hollywood Court to check on Hakim, but Hakim wasn't home. He found Cristal and Kee-Kee sitting in the living room, drinking Hennessy and tripping over how Todd had beaten MT down. Todd had walked in on their conversation and ended up staying there for hours. Hakim never showed up, and Todd wasn't about to call and interrupt whatever might have been going on.

As he'd gotten up to walk out the door, Cristal had run up behind him, saying she wanted to spend the night with him. Just the thought had Todd really feeling good, so he'd told her to follow him in her Chrysler 300 to his father's mini-mansion. There, Todd had sexed Cristal up until she'd dozed off to sleep.

"Well, I'm happy I pleased you, baby girl," he said, kissing her soft lips. Then Todd lay back down next to her. He grabbed her by the hip and pulled her closer to his chest.

They both remained naked under the silk sheets, softly touching each other and heavily breathing in unison—a passion reserved only for lovers.

When the feeling of Cristal's warm body against his alerted his manhood, she noticed. Her lustful eyes locked on Todd's handsome face as he slightly bit down on his lip. "I've got to use the bathroom," she said.

Todd's eyes widened in surprise. "Come on! Now?"

"Boy, I'll be back. Just be patient," she said, rolling out of the king-sized bed, with ass everywhere.

Todd lay back on the pillow and placed both hands behind his head. He stared at the ceiling, waiting. "Hurry up, girl!" Todd said, feeling joyful and excited. He hopped out of bed, put on his red Polo boxer shorts, then reached into the ashtray on the nightstand to fetch the half-blunt he had left over from the night before. He then grabbed the lighter out of his pants pocket and sat at the edge of the bed to smoke. As

Todd slowly inhaled the weed smoke, thoughts of Beautiful overwhelmed any excitement or joy he had in his heart about Cristal. Being in the presence of Beautiful had allowed him to go beyond the beauty of her skin and into the mind of bliss. Beautiful was, from what Todd had learned, a good female—someone he'd consider giving his love and heart to. He'd also found out that she was studying to become a doctor which only made him more interested.

Todd's thoughts of Beautiful were interrupted when Cristal stepped out of the bathroom and walked toward him. "So tell me, Todd, where do we stand as of now?" she asked, standing there bow-legged in front of him.

"What do you mean?" he said, exhaling.

Cristal placed her hands on her hips. "Todd, you know what I mean! I want to know if last night was just a one-night fuck or what."

He put the blunt back in the ashtray and looked at her. "Shit no! You are my baby. Now bring yo' sexy ass here."

She blushed.

Todd grabbed her by the forearm and placed his hand on her stomach.

"I love the way you touch me, Todd."

"Is that right? Just wait until I put this dick in you."

"Oh, yes! I want it, Todd."

Todd removed his boxers, grabbed Cristal by the hand and escorted her into the shower with the sliding glass doors.

Cristal stepped in front of the shower sprinkler, and water ran down between her double-D breasts as she gently ran her fingers around the core of her wetness. She then reached back and grabbed Todd's manhood, until he became aroused. She placed her hands on the wall in front of her and bent over.

Todd slowly allowed his penis to penetrate her wetness while sprinkling water rolled down her bottom.

"Yessss! Yes…right there, Todd. Fuck—" Her words became caught up when Todd lifted her bottom and bent his knees. She moaned repeatedly, "Mmm…Todd! Go deeper, baby…"

Todd started breathing heavily as he fulfilled her every command. He pulled his penis out of her, then turned her around and lifted her up.

Cristal wrapped her legs around Todd's waist.

With water dripping from their bodies, Todd carried her back into the bedroom and laid her on the bed.

"I want you to fuck me in the ass," said Cristal, getting on her hands and knees.

Todd grinned, finding that surprising. He pulled her to the edge of the bed and slowly eased his penis into her tight, wet anus.

She tried to crawl away, but Todd gripped her hips tightly. "Oh, hell naw! You won't get away from me," he said, giving her every inch of his manhood. Cristal began to moan at the top of her lungs. When she saw that Todd wasn't going to allow her to pull away, she began throwing her rectum back into his penis, fulfilling her every desire.

Todd pulled his penis out of her anus and entered her vagina. Within five strokes, he exploded inside her like an erupting volcano.

Cristal looked back at Todd with a surprised expression on her face. "Boy, you just came inside of me! What if I get pregnant?"

He stepped back from her, holding his penis in his hand. "I'll take good care of it."

"We've got a whole life ahead of us. Besides, I'm not ready to be a mother just yet."

"It's all good, Cristal. I won't leave you, I got you. I got to be going though. What do you have planned for today?"

She lay back on the bed. "After I get done with my job interview at 2:00, I guess I'll go by Kee-Kee's house and kick it for a while."

"Okay. When I get finished handling my business, I should be able to drop by Hollywood Court." Todd kissed Cristal, then walked into the bathroom to get ready for the day.

* * *

After Cristal left, Todd took a quick shower, got dressed, and changed the sheets on the bed. He walked into the kitchen to grab a bite to eat before leaving. Man, I gotta call my mama, he thought, looking over at the pictures on the wall, photos of Money and Todd's mother. He picked up the cordless phone from the kitchen counter and dialed his mother's number.

Ms. Jackie answered on the third ring. "Hello?"

"Hey there, Mama."

"Oh, hey, baby!" she said with excitement in her voice.

"Todd grabbed a bottle of SunnyD from the refrigerator and drank from it. "I'm just calling to check up on you."

"Oh. Well, I'm fine, sweetie. So…how's college going?"

He leaned on the marble counter and held the phone to his ear. "I am loving it at the moment. The professor has taught me about services, retail, zoning, and manufacturing in small business."

"Wow! That's a plus in what you are trying to accomplish. Have you found the exact area where you want to put your club? I'm only asking because there're a lot of competition out here."

Todd ran his fingers through his neatly trimmed goatee. "That's my last worry, Mama. I have found a very good area on the East Side though. I'm in the process of getting this white boy I know to start a website for me so I can post ads and promote myself."

"Well, I'd say you're on the right track, and I hope the best for you, baby. Has your father gotten back into town?"

"Not yet. Hey, Mama, I'm on my way over to your house. Did you cook breakfast yet?"

"Yes," she said in her motherly voice. "Hakim is over here sleeping on my couch. His crazy butt came to my house drunk last night, so I took his car keys and made him stay."

Todd started laughing. "I went by his house looking for him last night."

"Do you want me to wake him up?"

"No! I'm on my way now though."

"All right. Bye, baby."

"Bye, Mama." He hung up the phone, walked into the living room, and grabbed the .380 pistol from under the seat cushions.

* * *

Outside, Todd hopped into Money's Benz. He had to make two quick stops before going to his mother's house in College Park.

He pulled first into a Chevron gas station, right off of Martin Luther King Jr. Drive. There were a few crack-heads and drug dealers standing on the corner making transactions.

The sun was at its highest, shining brightly.

Todd parked right in front of the gas pump, then hopped out, looking like a brand new $100 bill. Just as he walked up to the door to pay for his gas, a short, stocky, gray-headed black crack-head with ashes on his lips stepped up to Todd with his hand out. Todd looked him up and down. "I will give you some change when I come out of the store," he said.

"Okay. Thank you, sir."

Todd strolled over to the tall Arab who was standing behind the cash register. He handed the man $30. "Put that on Pump 23 please," he said, then walked back out the door.

The crack-head saw Todd walking toward his car and ran up behind him. "Here I am, sir."

Todd turned around and gave the fiend a $10 bill. "You can have this, but I want you to pump my gas for it."

Without another word, the crack-head ran over to the gas pump, placed the nozzle in the tank, and started pumping.

Todd jumped in the Benz and called Beautiful from his cell phone.

"Hello?" she answered.

"What's up, shawty?" he asked, leaning back in the driver seat.

"Oh! Hey, boo! Why didn't I see you during first period? I was looking forward to seeing you."

Todd's conversation with Beautiful was interrupted when the crack-head tapped the window. "Hold on, baby girl." Todd placed the phone against his chest, then pressed the button to roll the power window down.

The crack-head knelt down. "I'm finished, sir. Thank you for the 10 bucks."

"No problem. Just spend it on the right thing," Todd

calmly said before he pulled into traffic with the phone held up to his ear. "Yeah, so what's good with you, Beautiful?"

"Nothing much. Who was that you were talking to?"

Todd drew in a breath. "Some old crack-head who I had pumping my gas."

"Oh, okay. So…why haven't I seen you today?"

"I overslept, and it was your fault," he lied, saying the first thing that came to mind.

Beautiful laughed. "How was it my fault?"

"You knew it would be hard for me to leave your room once I saw you."

She continued to laugh into the receiver. "Boy, stop."

"So, when's your next class?" Todd asked, making a left turn off the expressway."

"It's at 2:30. Why do you ask?"

"I wanted to stop by and get a kiss."

"Hmm. Is that right? Well, I guess I could meet you in front of the college."

"Sounds good to me. I'm on the way now."

"I'll see you then," said Beautiful.

"All right," Todd stated as he ended the call.

He pressed the play button on the CD player and continued cruising down the street with a look of excitement on his face. Al Green's "Love and Happiness" came through the speakers, echoing his mood. Todd laid back in the driver seat and kept one hand on the steering wheel. The thought of kissing Beautiful sent a chill down his spine. For the first time in his life, he had allowed a woman to captivate the feelings he'd hidden so well.

SCHOOL BOY

* * *

Within minutes, Todd was pulling into Clark Atlanta College, with his music blaring loud. Beautiful wasn't where she had said she'd be, so Todd decided to sit on the hood of the Benz until she showed up.

Just as he was reaching in the car for his cell phone to call her, Beautiful came walking through the double doors, dressed in hot pink capri pants, pink D&G body suit that showed her belly ring, and pink, open-toed stiletto heels. She was even wearing pink eyeliner, matching lip gloss, and pink fingernail polish, and her hair was pulled back in a long ponytail.

A pleased glimmer sparked in Todd's eyes. He reached into the glove compartment and grabbed a small fourteen-karat gold necklace that he brought along with him that had a heart shaped diamond charm on it. Todd had been holding on to the necklace for nearly two and a half years. He'd promised himself that when he finally found that special woman in his life, he would give it to her. Todd felt that Beautiful was unique in many ways, and whenever he was in her presence, he felt relaxed. "Here. This is for my queen," he said, holding the necklace in the palm of his hand.

She began to blush, then placed her hand over her mouth. "I-I don't know what to say. Thank you, Todd."

"You don't have to thank me. When I give, it's from the heart," Todd quickly replied, leaning against his car door.

Beautiful embraced Todd and gave him a wet kiss on the lips. "You're so sweet."

Todd grabbed her by both arms.

Beautiful looked puzzled. "What's wrong?" she asked.

"Promise me you'll always be by my side, no matter what," he said with an expression that showed how serious he was.

She stepped closer to Todd; her stare indicated she was serious as well. "Todd, I really do believe in you and everything you told me last night. Just don't break my heart, and I won't abandon you."

"I won't." He hugged her very tightly. "Check this out, my queen. I gotta go by my mama's house now, but how about I take you to the movies tonight?"

She smiled. "I would love that! What time will you pick me up?"

"Around 8 o'clock."

"I'll be ready."

They kissed each other.

As Todd hopped into the Benz and pulled off, he looked in the rearview mirror. Beautiful was still standing in the parking lot, examining the necklace.

* * *

Todd pulled up at the red light feeling great. His phone rang all of the sudden, and he used his earpiece to answer the call. "Hello?"

"When were you going to call me, handsome?" a soft voice said from the other end.

"Who is this?"

"This is Alexus. We met by the water fountain at school, remember?"

"Oh yeah! Ms. Bow-leg. What it do, sexy?"

"Just got out of class. I thought you were going to take me out?"

Todd had a joker's smile on his face. "I'm sorry, but I've been really busy. Can I call you later, because I'm in a business meeting right now," he lied, just so he could get off the phone.

"That's fine. I'll be waiting."

"I got ya."

"Bye, Todd."

He hung up without responding. Damn! I forgot about that little ho! he thought to himself, realizing he was starting to lose track.

* * *

Todd turned off of the expressway and took a left down Flat Shoals until he came to a four-way stop sign. As Todd cruised through the neighborhood, he noticed a group of kids playing football in the streets, just as he used to do when he was a boy. Todd slowed down as he took a trip down Memory Lane, thinking back to his childhood days, good times spent with friends. At his mother's house, he parked behind Hakim's Buick Regal.

Ms. Jackie stepped out the front door, still dressed in her nightgown. She still looked sexy and young, despite her fifty-two years. Her caramel-colored hair was wet and tangled from her shower. She had kept her figure toned and inviting through years of yoga, her skin was still smooth, and she had those dreamy, grab-you-and-never-let-you-go hazel eyes. She just stood in front of her chrome and black two-tone Harley Davidson F-150 and said, "Took you long enough." There was joy in her eyes at seeing her son again.

"I had to make a stop…and I love you too, Mama." He

gave her a hug.

"Where's Hakim?"

"His butt is in there."

Todd escorted his mother back into the house. From the front door to the kitchen, the living room had thick brown carpet. There were two matching leather couches, one in each corner, and a large fish tank filled with colorful, tropical fish, sitting on a stand right next to the stereo system. Pictures of Todd filled the walls.

Hakim came strolling out of the kitchen with a glass of orange juice in his hand.

"What's the move, shawty?" asked Todd, sitting on the loveseat.

After Ms. Jackie walked into the kitchen, Hakim gave Todd some dap and took a seat on the couch closest to the window. "What's up, brah?"

"Mama told me you came in drunk last night."

Hakim scooted to the edge of the cushion. "Shawty, that li'l ho Peaches is off the mother-fucking chain."

Todd grinned. "I went by your house looking for you last night. I thought about calling you when I didn't find you there, but Cristal was over there with Kee-Kee. You already know how that went down."

"Okay then, young pimping. Peep the move, shawty. Stay on point with that nigga MT."

Todd's face curled into a frown. "Fuck that pussy nigga! He gon' fuck around and bring the beast out of me."

"Brah, I'm with you to the end. I'm just sayin' we may have to put them pistols on this nigga. Right now, you got school to finish, and you may not be ready."

"Shawty, you'd be surprised what I'm ready for," Todd

said in a low voice.

"Niggas don't fight these days."

Todd stood to his feet with a frown still on his face. When he was mad, he looked just like his father, Money Mac. "I ain't talking about fighting, brah. I'm talking about a possible murder if this nigga come fucking with me!"

"What you two talking about in here?" Ms. Jackie asked when she returned to the room holding two plates full of pancakes, eggs, and bacon. "Here y'all go. If you want more, there's plenty on the stove."

Hakim grabbed the plate and smiled. "Thank you, Mama!"

"Boy, you don't have to thank me. Todd, I got to get dressed so I can go pay some bills. Make sure you and Hakim lock up when you leave."

"Okay, Mama," Todd said with a mouthful of food.

Ms. Jackie strolled up the flight of stairs to get dressed, and Todd and Hakim began to dig into their breakfast.

"Shawty, me and Chris fucked that ho Peaches," Hakim said, placing his plate on his lap.

"For real?"

"Hell yeah."

"I went by her friend's room, and we kicked it for a good li'l minute."

Hakim looked as if he had no idea who Todd was talking about. "Kicked it with who, shawty?"

Todd glanced over at him. "C'mon, shawty!"

"What, pimp?"

"You know—that li'l ho who was fucking with that lame-ass nigga MT."

"Oh yeah," Hakim stated with a smile and a nod. "That's why old boy approached you, huh, shawty?"

"Hell yeah."

"So…did you fuck the bitch?"

"Nah. I did not fuck Beautiful. All we did was kick it."

Hakim stared at Todd silently, and his eyes narrowed. "Are you falling for her already?"

"What?"

"You heard me."

Todd's cheeks puffed out a blast of air. "Be real, shawty. Me, falling for a bitch, is like my dad retiring from the pimp game. Just ain't gon' happen. What makes you ask that anyway?"

"No reason. But, hey, I gotta get going so I can get this money," Hakim said as he walked to the kitchen with his plate.

Ms. Jackie came down the stairs, fumbling through her purse for her car keys. "Baby, I'm goin'. Don't forget to lock up. The extra house key is hanging in the key holder in the kitchen. Give me a hug before I leave."

Todd walked over to his mother with the plate in his hand and hugged her tightly.

Ms. Jackie then smiled at them both and walked out the side door that led to the garage, and the sound of a dog barking echoed through the room. Suddenly, she peeked her head back through the door and yelled for Todd.

He came running through the kitchen in a hurry, breathing hard.

Ms. Jackie started laughing when she saw how fast Todd had come to the door. "Boy, why are you running through my house?"

"I heard a dog barking and you calling me. I thought something was wrong."

Hakim walked up behind Todd, his hands still wet from

rinsing his plate in the sink. "What's going on in here?"

"Nothing. I was just calling Todd in here to ask him to feed Princess."

"Princess?" Todd asked, pushing the door open.

Money's red-nosed pit bull came rushing toward Todd, wiggling her tail. "Uh, Money, uh…"

"What's wrong, baby?"

Money told me to look after her, and I forgot."

Ms. Jackie nodded. "That's why he brought her by here before he left. He knew you would forget with all you've got going on."

Todd knelt down on one knee, and Princess ran into his arms and licked him in the face. "After I feed her, I'ma head out myself."

Ms. Jackie pressed the button to open the garage door, then hopped into her pearl-white Escalade and rolled down the power window. "Love you, baby," she shouted before she backed out of the drive way.

"Love you too, Mom." Todd waved.

Hakim grabbed his Smith & Wesson .45 handgun from under the couch. "Todd, I'ma catch up with you later."

"You goin'?" Todd yelled over the sound of the barking dog.

"Hell yeah."

"Check. I'll see you later then."

Hakim walked out the front door with his gun wrapped in his shirt.

After Todd fed Princess, he washed his plate in the sink, then walked out the door.

CHAPTER 7

The Clark Atlanta campus was packed with students, mingling, sitting under the trees studying, or laughing and joking around. Todd looked at his Rolex watch and saw that it was 3 o'clock. He pulled into the parking lot, parked behind a green Honda, and hopped out.

Since it was still early, he decided to go to his dorm for a while. Todd entered the room and saw that Richard was gone, so he walked over to the bed and lay down, placing his hands behind his head.

Within minutes, Todd was sound asleep, and he didn't wake up until a tap on his leg startled him. "What the fuck?" he replied, jumping to his feet.

Richard stepped back with both hands in the air. "Dude! It's me. You were tossing and turning again, so I woke you."

Todd wiped the sweat from his forehead, then looked at his watch. "Oh shit!"

"What's wrong, dude?"

"Nothing. I gotta get going though. It's 7:30 already." Todd couldn't believe how time had gone by so quickly.

Richard strolled into the bathroom while Todd walked out the front door.

* * *

When he got to the parking lot, Beautiful and Peaches were standing next to the Benz, talking.

Peaches pointed at Todd when she saw him approaching. "There he go, girl," she said.

Beautiful had her back turned to him, and she slowly turned around, only to find Todd standing before her, smiling.

"Are you ready to go to the movies, baby girl?"

"Yes," she said, blushing.

"Todd?" a soft voice cried out from behind him.

Todd immediately turned to acknowledge the familiar voice. Keisha and two other girls were sitting on the hood of a purple Infiniti with the music playing.

"Oh. Hey there, um…" he said, trying to remember her name."

"It's Keisha!" she quickly responded.

Todd snapped his fingers. "Yeah, that's it. What's good with you, Keisha?"

Beautiful and Peaches looked at each other. "I know that bitch see us standing here," said Beautiful, rolling her eyes.

Peaches touched Beautiful on the arm. "Girl, fuck that bitch. You too sexy and beautiful for that ho. She got to get on your level."

Keisha noticed the two of them staring her down with a look of jealousy, but she fought to pay them no mind and kept talking to Todd. "Why haven't you been in class all day?"

Before he could reply, Beautiful stepped in front of him. "Because he been with me," she said, rolling her neck.

When Todd saw that talking to Keisha was going to be a problem, he grabbed Beautiful by the forearm. "Keisha, this my girl Beautiful, and baby, this is Keisha, my classmate. She showed me around the campus on my first day here," he said, trying to bring some peace before things got out of hand.

Keisha's eyes widened in surprise, because Todd had tried to talk to her. "I'm sorry. No disrespect, Beautiful," she said, holding back her anger.

"Don't be, girl. I was wrong for overreacting so quickly toward you," she apologized with a smirk on her face. Then Beautiful turned and kissed Todd on the cheek. "Baby, I'm sorry," she softly replied, wearing a puppy-dog face.

Todd looked down into her eyes. "Don't be, my queen. Tonight is your night. Are you ready to head out?"

"Yes. Peaches, girl, I will call you later."

"Bye, girl. I hope y'all have a good time at the movies."

"We will," Todd said, and they both jumped in the Benz and pulled off.

Peaches stood on the grass until Todd's taillights were out of sight.

* * *

The Greenbriar Mall parking lot was jam-packed when Todd pulled in. The line to the movie theater wasn't that crowded; there were only a few teenagers waiting for their tickets to get in.

"What do you want to see?" Todd asked as they walked toward the ticket booth, holding hands.

Beautiful looked up and down at the posters and the movie listings, searching for the perfect thing to watch together. "Ooh, baby! Let's see Safe House. I hear Denzel Washington plays the fuck out of his role in that."

Todd strolled up to the booth and paid for two tickets. Two young black girls, who looked like they were still in high school, stared Todd down from their place in line. Beautiful peeped them out, and without delay, she stepped behind Todd and put her hand in his back pocket.

The movie ended at 9:30, and Todd stopped by a BP gas station to fill up before dropping Beautiful off at the college campus.

It had been a great day for Todd and Beautiful, and for the first time in their lives, love had presented itself.

Todd stopped in front of Pump 8.

"Ain't that some shit?" Beautiful asked.

"What's wrong?"

"That's MT in that red Dodge Viper parked beside us."

Todd reached under the driver seat for the .380 handgun and placed it in his waistband. "Fuck him."

"Don't you do anything crazy, baby."

"I won't. Just sit tight, and I'll be right back."

"Can I pump yo' gas?"

Todd smiled. "Yeah. You do that. Represent for me, baby girl." Then Todd got out of the car and walked into the gas station without being seen by MT.

Beautiful stepped out of the Benz, strutting proudly in her hot pink capri pants and open-toed stiletto heels.

MT spotted her and noticed the sexy stance she had while she leaned over the trunk of Todd's car. He climbed out of his Viper and started walking toward her with a look that could have killed on contact.

Todd watched from inside to see how Beautiful would handle the situation.

"What's good, Beautiful?" MT said, grabbing her by the

forearm.

Beautiful yanked her arm away from his grip. "Don't you fucking touch me!"

"Don't play with me, for real. You'll always be my bitch."

"Bitch? Pussy nigga, yo' mama's the bitch!"

MT bit down on his bottom lip, clenching his fist tight. "Watch your mouth, ho, before I put my fist in it."

"You better not hit me." Beautiful's eyes filled with terror as she looked around for Todd.

MT looked back in the same direction as Beautiful was looking and saw Todd standing inside the gas station, observing the whole scene with a smile on his face. "See? I knew you was fucking that nigga. He got you pumping his gas and everything. I got something for his bitch ass. You let him know that." MT walked back to his car and pulled off, leaving a smokescreen behind.

Todd started laughing when he got in the car. He put the gun back under the seat and waited for Beautiful to finish pumping gas. When she hopped in the passenger seat, Todd started the engine and pulled off.

He and Beautiful remained silent for a moment, but then Beautiful looked over at Todd; she saw something in Todd's eyes that wasn't sitting well with her. "That's a crazy-ass man," Beautiful stated.

"Who?" he asked, knowing good and well whom she was referring to.

"MT, baby."

"Fuck that nigga! Whatever he going through, he'll get over it."

Beautiful forced a tight smile. "Baby…"

"Yes, my queen?"

"It's nothing." Beautiful wanted to tell Todd what MT had said, about the threat he'd made, but she decided to keep it to herself just to keep confusion down.

Todd looked puzzled, but he kept his eyes on the road. "Damn. So we doing it like that now?"

"What, baby?"

"Don't trip it," Todd stated, turning up the music.

Beautiful glanced outside the window, praying that MT was only talking when he told her he was going to get Todd.

It was late and dark when Todd pulled into the Clark Atlanta parking lot. Hakim and Peaches were sitting on the hood of Hakim's Buick Regal, smoking a marijuana blunt. Todd parked in an empty spot two cars down, and he and Beautiful, still holding hands, walked over to greet their friends.

"Hey, girl!" Beautiful greeted, while Todd gave Hakim some dap.

Peaches leapt to her feet and hugged Beautiful. "Girl, what'd y'all see?"

"Safe House."

"Ooh! I heard that movie's good," Peaches said with excitement.

"It was," Beautiful said, yawning and holding her hand up to her mouth.

Peaches looked back at Hakim. "Boo, are you going to take me to see Safe House?"

Hakim passed Todd the blunt before responding, "I got ya, li'l mama."

"Todd, walk me to my room. I'm tired as hell," said Beautiful.

"Girl, you know that punk-ass security guard is sitting

right at the front desk tonight," Peaches warned.

"I'm tired of that fat-ass security guard. He got the nerve to try to get at me, girl."

Peaches started laughing. "Girl, you crazy! That's why me and Hakim was sitting out here talking."

"Well, come on, Todd. Walk me to the front door then." She grabbed Todd by the hand.

Todd escorted Beautiful to the front door and gave her a kiss. He watched her walk through the doors. Damn. She's fine as hell, he thought, licking his lips. As Todd walked away, his cell phone began to ring. "Yeah? Who's speaking?" he asked, feeling good about himself.

"Where are you, boy?" asked Money Mac.

"Oh shit! What's up, Dad? I'm on the college campus with Hakim."

"Come by the house so we can change whips. I'ma buy you a new car next week."

"Okay. I'm on the way now."

"Put Hakim on the phone."

"Hold on." Todd walked over to Hakim, who was kissing Peaches on the neck. "Here, brah."

"Who is this?" he asked, with the phone held against his chest.

"Money."

Hakim pushed Peaches to the side and walked to the trunk of his car. "What's good, Money?"

"Nothing much, young pimpin'. Peep the move. I got some new shit, straight off the ship. When you're ready, let me know."

"Oh, hell yeah! I gotta get some of that ASAP. I thought you weren't comin' back till next week though."

"I know. Me and Grip decided to come back early."

"I'll be getting at you soon, boss man."

"Okay. Give Todd the phone."

"Bet that." Hakim walked back to the front and handed the phone to Todd.

"I'll be there in a few," Todd said to his dad.

"All right, son," Money stated, then hung up.

Hakim looked over at Todd. "Hey, brah, are you going over there?" he asked.

"Yeah. Y'all two be easy," Todd said, throwing up the peace sign.

Hakim rubbed Peaches on the knee gently, then opened his car door. "I got to get going, baby girl. I'ma get with you later."

She kissed her hand, then blew it at Hakim as he hopped in the car. "Call me, boo!"

CHAPTER 8

Money Mac's Monte Carlo SS was parked behind Jay-Bo's Mercedes-Benz ML63. Todd parked at the front gate, right next to the mailbox. He used his key to open the front door and found Grip sitting in the white La-Z-Boy chair, rolling up a blunt. To his right, Jay-Bo and GG sat at the small bar, drinking a glass vodka and smoking a cigarette.

There were two 9mm Glock handguns lying on the glass table, three briefcases filled with cash, a Gucci suitcase that contained $1 million in cash, and six duffel bags with sixty-five kilos of pure Peruvian cocaine lying on the floor.

Grip, Jay-Bo, and GG turned their heads toward Todd when the front door closed.

"What's good, young Todd?" asked Grip.

"Nothing much on my end. What's good with you?"

"Getting ready to fire up this Jamaican kush."

Todd looked over at GG and Jay-Bo, then back at Grip. "Where's my dad?"

Grip held the blunt up to his lips and lit it, then pointed toward the kitchen where Money was.

Todd nodded his head, then walked toward the kitchen in there to find Money.

"Todd!" Jay-Bo said, stepping down from the barstool,

his eyes bloodshot.

Todd turned around. "What's up?" he asked, with his hand covering his belt buckle.

"Don't you fuck with Hakim from Hollywood Court?"

"Hell yeah! That's my brother. Who are you?"

"Shawty, I'm Jay-Bo, and that's my brother, GG."

Todd looked at GG and threw up the peace sign with his fingers. "Are you the same Jay-Bo who got the whole West Side on lock with the kush?"

Jay-Bo smiled. "That will be me. Come by my spot and get at me sometimes. I seen you around the 'hood, but I never knew you was Money's son. I keep that good shit, so stop by—free of charge for you."

"That's what's up!" Todd stated. He gave Jay-Bo some dap, then walked into the kitchen.

* * *

When Todd walked in, Money Mac was sitting at a large glass table, drinking a glass of Patrón and rotating two silver meditation balls in his hand. Money often used the balls when he was trying to concentrate on some important business. Todd knew something was troubling his father because of the way he was moving the mediation balls around through his hands and fingers.

"Take a seat, Todd," Money said, without even turning to look at Todd.

Todd looked surprised. "How did you know it was me?"

"Boy, I know you didn't just ask me that. Who else come in my house smelling like a half-bottle of Polo Sport body wash?" Money asked with a smirk. "And if you were a killer coming to off me, I would have smelled you from a mile away."

Todd took a seat across from Money. He had a serious look on his face.

"You know I love you, right?" Money asked, looking over at his son.

"Sure I do. What makes you ask that?"

Money placed the two balls in a large box, then leaned over the table from the place where he was seated. "Now, you listen to me. Always remember that a man whose mind is not open to reality will fail in whatever it is he's trying to accomplish. Continue to be a leader and treat your fellow man well. They're putting their lives on the line for you."

Todd's lips remained sealed as he allowed Money's words to settle in his mind.

Money took a sip from his glass, then sat back in his seat. "Do you understand?"

"I got you," said Todd.

"Come with me."

They both walked into the living room.

"Do you see these three men right here?" Money pointed at Jay-Bo, Grip, and GG.

Todd nodded.

"If anything ever happens to me, you can always turn to them for help."

Todd focused intently on all three men.

"Do you still have the gun I gave you?" Money asked, setting his glass down.

"Yeah. I keep it on me," Todd replied, pulling out the .380 from his waistband and laying it down on the mantel.

Money, Jay-Bo, Grip, and GG smiled at the same time.

"Hey, Jay-Bo!" Money yelled.

"What's good?"

"Give my son something better than that .380."

"I got ya, Todd. Just come by Simpson Houses tomorrow around 3:00 p.m."

"Okay. Give me your cell number so I can lock it in my phone," Todd said, whipping out his cellular phone from its black leather case.

"It's 404-831-1217. Call me."

"Hey, Jay-Bo…" Todd said.

"Yeah?"

"Do you know a nigga named MT?" he asked as he laid the pistol on the small glass table and put his cell phone back in its holder on his belt.

"Yeah. He's one of my workers from Candler Road. Why you ask?"

GG turned around from the bar, while Grip inhaled marijuana smoke through his nose.

"He want beef with me."

A frown appeared on Money's face. "What you mean, he want beef with you?" he asked in a strong, deep voice. When it came to anybody messing with Todd, Money didn't play the radio.

"I had to beat his ass because he came to me talking about a bitch who don't even want his lame ass."

"Well, I shoulda known that," said Money.

"Damn, li'l Todd! You taking them niggas' hoes?" Grip yelled from the La-Z-Boy where he was sitting.

Todd smiled.

"Don't trip on that nigga, Todd. I'll get at him," GG said.

"Naw, it's all good. I can handle it myself," Todd quickly

responded.

"Are you sure?"

"Hell yeah!"

Money Mac took another sip of the half-full glass of Patrón, then licked his lips. "Todd, check this out. How many times I told you not to keep fighting with these niggas? Now, if you want to be a boxer, jump your ass in a ring, but out here in the real world, gunfire rules. You can't keep putting yo' hands up everywhere you have beef with a nigga. The generation now don't respect an ass-kicking," Money said, walking behind the bar and grabbing the whole bottle of Patrón. "And another thing, you will have a new car soon. Let me say this to you, son. It's cool you're in college and shit, but you ain't no baby no more. It's time for you to start getting some money of your own. Yo' mama said she wants to put down on a ride for you and asked me to pay the notes. I'll pay two notes, but that's it. I risked my life out there to get this bread, so now you gotta step up and show the world you can get money without me," Money said, then walked over to a duffel bag and pulled out two kilos of pure Peruvian cocaine. "Here. Each one of these bricks cost anywhere from $80,000 to $90,000 because it's still pure. It can take a hell of a cut. Go get your money, son."

Todd stared at the two kilos of cocaine blankly as he held them in his hands. He began to get nervous, because selling drugs wasn't his thing. Besides, who am I supposed to sell it to? he thought. Coming up as a kid, Todd had always depended on his father to take care of him, but times had changed, and it was time for Todd to step out on his own and get money the best way he knew how. Then, all of a sudden, as he thought it over, a smile appeared on his face; he had a plan. "Well, fellas, I'ma holla at y'all. I gotta get going. And, Jay-Bo, I will stop by your spot around 4:00 tomorrow, after I get out of class."

"Here, son. Take the Monte Carlo SS," Money said, tossing Todd the car keys.

"Okay. Be easy, Grip and GG.

They both responded at the same time with a smile and a nod.

Todd walked out the front door, leaving his .380 behind. He hopped in the Monte Carlo, stuffed the two kilos partially under the passenger seat, and turned the ignition.

Just as Todd grabbed the steering wheel, his cell phone started ringing. When he looked at the caller ID, he saw that it was Cristal. "Hello?" he answered.

"Can you come get me?" Her voice was soft and calm.

"Where are you?"

"At home in Sandy Springs."

"Okay. Text the address to my phone so I can put it into my navigation system."

"I'm sending it now."

"Cristal…"

"Yeah, baby?"

"Can I spend some time with you tonight?" Todd asked, hoping she picked up on his insinuation of having a more intimate night.

"Yes you can, baby."

"Okay. See you soon," Todd said, and then he hung up.

* * *

An hour later, Todd was pulling up in the driveway of Cristal's house. She came out the door wearing her sky-blue capri pants, a white t-shirt that said "Got Dick?", blue sunglasses, and open-toed heels that showed off her beautiful pedicure.

"You ready, baby girl?" Todd asked as he stepped out of the car.

"Damn, Todd. Is this your car too?"

"Naw. The Benz I was driving before and this one are my dad's. Somebody stole mine that day I saw you at the mall."

"For real?" she said, jumping into the passenger seat.

Todd got back behind the wheel. "It was probably one of them lame-ass niggas from Vine City, because they be hanging around the West End a lot."

"Well, I'm sorry to hear that, baby. I hope you find it."

"It's cool. I'll have a new ride soon," he said, backing out of the driveway.

"I know you will."

"Hey, baby girl, let's get a room at the Holiday Inn."

She looked over at Todd out of the corner of her eye and smiled. "Sounds good to me, handsome."

It was 11 o'clock when Todd and Cristal arrived at the Holiday Inn in College Park. The parking lot was half full, and Todd left Cristal in the car while he went in to pay for the room. He walked through the glass double doors that led to the front desk in the lobby. Three women were standing at the front desk, waiting for the keys to their room, and Todd stood behind them. "Excuse me, ladies," he said, licking his lips like LL Cool J.

"Yes?" they replied at the same time, all with lust in their eyes.

"Are y'all in line?"

They stepped to the side. "Oh no handsome. We are waiting to get our key so we can go swimming in that indoor pool."

"That's what's up," he said, walking up to the front desk.

The three girls stared Todd up and down, but he paid them no further mind.

"May I help you, sir?" the old white clerk said.

"Yes. I need a room for me and my girl," he said, loud enough so the three women would know he was not alone.

"Okay, sir. Please let me see your ID."

"I'd like a room on the third floor, please," he said, handing her his driver's license.

The cashier walked over to the computer and typed in Todd's info. "That will be $59.99, sir," she said.

Todd reached into his pocket and handed the cashier a $100 bill. She gave him back his change and a plastic keycard to unlock the room door.

When Todd stepped outside, the slight cool breeze of Atlanta greeted him. "What you doing, sexy lady?" Todd asked Cristal as he climbed inside the car.

"I was just listening to the weather station. There's a rainstorm coming."

"Really?"

"That's what the weather man said."

"Okay. Well, they gave us Room 323 on the third floor. Go on up there and order a pizza. I gotta make a quick run."

Cristal pouted, sticking out her bottom lip, and glared at Todd.

"Don't do that, baby girl. I'll be right back."

She hit Todd on the leg. "Boy, I was just playing with you. Go handle your business while I play with my pussy."

"No! Wait until I come back before you do that."

"Okay."

Todd leaned forward and kissed Cristal on the mouth. "That's just a li'l somethin' till I get back. Here's the card to unlock the door."

Cristal grabbed the keycard, ran her fingers through Todd's hair, then climbed out of the car.

* * *

Todd sped out of the parking lot, fumbling for his cellular on his hip. When he got to the red light, he punched in Chris's number on the speed dial. "C'mon. C'mon!" he said, impatiently waiting for the call to connect, but much to his dismay, he was greeted only by Chris's voicemail.

Just as the light turned green, Todd's phone started ringing. He looked at the screen and saw that it was Alexus. He tossed the phone over to the passenger seat and turned onto the expressway.

Forty-five minutes later, Todd was cruising down West Lake with his music turned up to the max. The night was silent, with a full moon. There was a slight chance of rain, from what Cristal had told him, and the wind was blowing around in the street. Crack-heads walked up and down the sidewalks like zombies, except instead of hungering for flesh, they were looking for their next hit of crack cocaine.

Todd pulled into the driveway of Chris's townhouse, which sat across from the Overlook Atlanta apartments. He parked behind a 2008 Chevrolet Silverado and blew the horn twice.

Chris came strolling out the front door, with his son Wāhid in his arms.

Todd turned down his music and stepped out of the car.

"What's good, brah?" Chris said, giving Todd some dap with his free hand.

"Ready to get to the money."

Chris sat Wāhid down on the porch. "Ain't we both! The li'l money I am making…hell, I have to spend it all on my son and bills. Oh yeah! Why did you beat old boy's ass the other night?"

"Shawty, fuck that nigga! I got some'n I need to show you. Can you ride with me for a minute?"

"Hell yeah. I need to get some apple-mango blunts from the store anyway," Chris said, picking up his son again to carry him into the house.

Todd stood on the porch, staring at the sky and waiting for Chris.

Within five minutes, Chris walked out the door, dressed in a black tank top, Rocawear jeans, all-black Jordans, and a pair of Giorgio Armani eyewear that blended in with his coconut complexion. He was still short, with low-cut hair and thick eyebrows. "You ready, shawty?" Chris asked, adjusting his belt buckle.

"Yeah. Let's ride," Todd said. After he and Chris hopped into the car, Todd said, "Shawty, reach under the seat and hand me that package."

Chris felt under the passenger seat, and his eyes grew big when he realized he was feeling kilos of cocaine, neatly wrapped in plastic. "Damn, nigga! You done come up!"

Todd smiled. "Naw, brah. We done come up. Are you ready to get money?"

"Fuck yeah! I know a few niggas who want some right now. We can sell the whole thing for $25,000?"

"Did you say $25,000? Shawty, that's pure Peruvian flake!"

Chris looked over at Todd, amazed. "Oh yeah?"

"Damn right."

"Shawty, where did you get this?"

Todd winked his eye, then reclined in his seat. "I got it from my dad. Now, don't ask why he gave it to me. Just know it's our time to come up."

"Fuck that! I'm going in the kitchen when I get back and cooking this shit up. We can whip this pure into four bricks and still sell each brick for like $25,000 or $26,000 a piece. Hold on a minute. Let me put these in the house. Riding around with this could get us both some federal time." Chris hopped out of the car with the two kilos and ran to the back of his house. Within seconds, he returned.

Todd grabbed the steering wheel with one hand and started his ignition with the other.

Chris jumped into the passenger seat, breathing hard, with his mouth open.

Todd pulled off at a slow pace because of the white Lexus that was cruising in front of him. "What the fuck wrong with this mother-fucker, driving all slow and shit?" Todd said, irritated.

"Shit! Drive around them, shawty."

Todd pressed his foot down on the gas and sped past the Lexus.

Chris turned up the volume on the CD player, and Li'l

Wayne's Carter IV played through the speakers.

The BP gas station parking lot was really busy, with cars running in and out, so Todd pulled into the Towers Liquor Store off Bankhead. There was a U-Haul truck with two black men in it parked in the far corner of the parking lot.

While Todd backed into his parking spot, Chris glanced over at the large crowd that stood in front of the Blue Flame Strip Club across the street.

"These young niggas hungry for the money around here," Todd said, looking over his shoulder at the four young drug dealers running to the blue Ford Taurus with crack rock cocaine in their hands.

Chris looked back himself. "Them young niggas so stupid, because all money ain't good money. That white man in that Ford Taurus looks like an undercover police officer, if ya ask me."

Todd activated the car alarm, and he and Chris walked into the liquor store.

The black Russell Simmons-looking manager stood behind the cash register, watching Todd and Chris as they walked down the aisle, shopping for alcohol.

Chris grabbed a bottle of Hennessy, then headed toward the front counter while Todd kept looking around. "Can I get a box of apple-mango blunts?" Chris asked, reaching into his pocket for his cash.

The manager placed a box of blunts on the counter. "Will that be it, sir?"

"Yes," Chris said, handing him a $50 bill.

"Okay. Your change sir. Have a good one."

"You too."

Todd walked up to the counter with a bottle of Grey

Goose vodka. He paid the manager, and then he and Chris walked out the front door. Todd noticed two young guys, around nineteen years old, looking in the window of his SS Monte Carlo. "Oh, hell naw! What the fuck y'all li'l niggas doing looking in my shit?" Todd asked in anger.

"Fuck you, nigga!" the two guys said, then took off running behind the store.

Chris started laughing as he and Todd opened their doors and placed the brown paper bags in the back seat.

Chris had his head down, opening the box of blunts.

Todd instinctively reached under the driver seat for his .380 handgun and realized it wasn't there. "Fuck!"

Chris looked over at Todd and saw two men with 9mm handguns creeping up on them. Before Chris could alert Todd of the danger, five shots sounded, and Todd fell forward in the driver seat. Chris was in a state of shock.

A voice yelled from in front of the store, "Are you all okay!"

Chris looked through the windshield and saw the store manager standing on the sidewalk with his .40 Glock aimed in the direction of the two gunmen.

Todd slowly opened his door and stood to his feet, and Chris was surprised to see him still alive, without a scratch on him. "What the fuck?" said Todd as he touched his body all over to make sure he hadn't been shot. He turned around and saw one of the robbers lying on the ground, moaning in a puddle of blood. The other one disappeared into the nights darkness.

"They've been around here all day trying to rob people," the liquor store manager said.

Todd looked over at him, and Chris stepped out of the car.

The crowd from across the street at the strip club began walking toward the scene to see who had been shot.

"They wouldn't have gotten shit," Chris replied.

"You two wait here. I gotta call the police and report this."

Chris and Todd walked over, inspected the wounded man then sat on the hood of the car as the manager walked back into the store.

Five minutes later, the police, paramedics and crime scene investigators were pulling up. They asked Todd and Chris a few questions, then let them go.

Todd dropped Chris off at the house, then headed back to the hotel.

* * *

When Todd got back to the Holiday Inn, he looked down at his Rolex and saw that it was 2:10 a.m. Todd spotted a vacant parking space right in front of the entrance that led to the third floor.

The incident that had occurred in front of the Towers Liquor Store played over again in Todd's head. He felt it was God giving him a wake-up call to take life more seriously than he had been. "How in the hell did I forget to grab my gun off the fireplace?" he mumbled, resting his head on the steering wheel.

Todd removed the keys from the ignition, grabbed his bottle of Grey Goose from the back seat, and got out of the car. Rain began to pour down hard from the dark sky, pelting Todd's head. He quickly dashed up the stairs rather than waiting on an elevator. By the time he got to the third floor, his clothes were soaking wet, and water was dripping from his braids.

Todd knocked lightly on the door, and Cristal immediately opened it with a look of concern etched on her face.

"Sorry it took me so long, baby girl," he said, stepping into the room.

"She folded her arms in disgust. "What too—"

He cut her off when he set the bottle of Grey Goose down on the table next to the window.

"I almost got killed tonight."

"What? How?"

"Me and Chris stopped by the Towers Liquor Store on Bankhead to grab something to drink. Two young niggas tried to rob us as we was coming out of the store. The store manager shot one of them and the other one got away."

"Oh my God!"

"The crazy part about it is, I left my gun over at my dad's house," he said, shaking his head and taking off his shirt. He tossed it to the floor.

Cristal unfastened his belt buckle and jeans, then slowly reached inside his boxer shorts and began stroking his penis until he came aroused. As soon as she saw that his manhood was rock hard, she got down on both knees and began licking around the tip of his penis.

Todd grabbed her lightly by the chin. "Hold on. Let's take this to the bed," he said. "You done got me horny as hell."

"What's the hurry?" she said, standing to her feet. "Let's drink that bottle of Grey Goose first."

Todd gave her a serious stare. "So you get me all hard, and now you want to drink before giving me some?"

"Yes, baby. I was just giving you a sample."

"Okay, whatever."

They walked over to the table and began drinking straight

from the bottle like two winos with a bottle of cheap whiskey.

Ten minutes later, the mattress springs were squeaking, the loud noise echoing through the room as Todd slowly stroked in and out of Cristal's wetness. "Whose pussy is this?" he asked.

"It's yours!" she screamed.

"Say it louder."

"I said it's yours, Daddy! It's all yours!"

"You're damn right it's mine. Now turn your ass over and spread your legs."

Todd flipped her onto her stomach in a doggy-style position and stroked her ass as hard as he could.

"Take it easy, baby. You're hurting me."

"It's supposed to hurt," he told her as sweat dripped from his forehead. "I'm gonna make sure you know without a doubt that this pussy's all mine!"

Cristal screamed so loud that the people in the room next door started beating on the wall. When Todd began to speed up, she used her hand as a brace to keep her head from banging against the wall. Todd thrust his 175-pound frame against her soft ass. She begged him to stop, but that only seemed to turn him on more.

"Stop whining! You know you love it, don't you?"

"Yes, baby, but you're punching a hole in my uterus!"

"Don't move. I'm cumming! I'm cumming!"

Cristal buried her face in the pillow and screamed as Todd jerked and shivered while his penis rested inside her wetness. When he was finished, she quickly rushed to the bathroom to take a shower. It was the first time a man had ever made her cum four times back to back.

Todd lay back comfortably on the king-sized bed and put

his hands behind his head, smiling and staring at the ceiling. Suddenly, his cellular phone over on the small table started ringing. "Who in the hell could be calling me at 4:00 in the morning?" he said to himself.

He grabbed his phone off the table next to the bed and checked to see who it was. The number on the screen showed up as Restricted, so Todd pressed ignore and laid the phone back on the table.

CHAPTER 9

Todd and Cristal checked out of the Holiday Inn at 1:00 p.m. He dropped her off at her house, because he was already twenty minutes late for class.

Todd pulled into the parking lot of Clark Atlanta College and parked his SS Monte Carlo behind Beautiful's red Escalade that her dad had bought for her the night before she'd started college. He looked down at his watch to see if he had enough time to take a quick shower before class ended. "I can make it," he said, hopping out of the car and running to his room.

When he got to the hallway, he saw his roommate walking toward the exit with his backpack hanging over his shoulder.

Todd had no time to speak to Richard, so he just walked right into the room. After taking a quick shower, Todd got dressed in his powder-blue Polo shorts set, white high-top Air Force 1 shoes, and powder-blue Atlanta fitted cap and headed out the door for class. His diamond and gold jewelry shone brightly when he stepped into the sun.

Todd was only forty minutes late when he walked into the classroom and took a seat in the rear. The teacher didn't even realize he'd been late, and he was really happy about that.

* * *

"Damn, it's hot!" Todd said when he stepped back out into the parking lot after class. "No wonder they call it Hotlanta."

Just as he was getting in the car, his cellular phone started ringing. "Hello?" he answered without looking at the caller ID.

"Hey, baby," said Ms. Jackie.

Todd sat on the hood of his SS Monte Carlo to take the call. "Oh, hey, Mama."

"Are you ready to go pick out a car for yourself?"

"Now?"

"Yes…now."

"Okay. Where do you want me to meet you?"

"In College Park, at Jones Dealership."

"I know where that is, but that place is high, Mama."

"Boy, I already talked with the owner. Let me handle that. Just be there."

"Okay. I'm on the way now."

"Love you."

"Love you too, Mama," he said before he hung up the phone.

"Todd!" a soft voice yelled from behind him.

When he turned around, Peaches was running through the parking lot, waving her hands in the air. Damn! What in the fuck do she want? Todd wondered as he reached in through the driver window and started the engine. "What's good, li'l buddy?" he asked, looking Peaches up and down.

"Me and Beautiful was talking last night. She told me to let you know that she's sorry."

Todd leaned against the driver door with a puzzled

expression on his face. "Why would she be sorry? I mean, what's she sorry for?"

Peaches took a deep breath before speaking. "She said she don't want you and MT beefing with each other over her."

"We're not beefing over her. Maybe he is, but I'm just defending myself."

"And that's why my girl's stressing."

"What? Over me defending myself?"

"No. To be all the way real with you. She said old boy wants to kill you."

Todd's heart rate started speeding—not because he was frightened, but because of the hidden excitement that lived within his soul. "Kill me?" he said, hopping into the car.

"Todd, please don't do anything crazy. Beautiful didn't want me to tell you, because she knew you would get mad."

"Peaches, you tell Beautiful I said we need to talk later. Right now, I'm headed to get me a car."

"That's what's up! I'll tell her."

Todd sped out of the parking lot in reverse, then whipped the car into drive like a stunt driver in some kind of action movie.

* * *

The sound of the duel exhaust pipes roared like a lion as Todd drove down Flatshoals in College Park, staring at the road ahead of him. The traffic wasn't jam-packed and hard to get through like it usually was, though there were a few taxi cabs escorting passengers to the airport.

Todd pulled into the circular parking lot of Jones Dealership. Ms. Jackie was standing next to a short white man, who looked to be in his mid-thirties, with a U.S. Marines crew cut and the stub of a big cigar clenched tightly in the corner of his mouth.

Todd parked behind a green drop-top 2013 Jaguar F-Type sports car. "Damn! This is the first Jaguar I've ever seen that looks like this," he said to himself as he jumped out of the car.

Ms. Jackie and the short white man walked over to where Todd stood. "Hey, baby," she said.

Todd turned around.

"This is Mr. Jones's son, and he will be helping you find what you need.

Todd's eyes lit up with joy, and then he smiled. "I already see what car I want."

The salesman stepped up to Todd with a clipboard in hand. "You do? Which one?" he asked.

"This Jag right here."

"Um…that's my father's car. It's not for sale."

The look on Ms. Jackie's face was completely serious. "I am not spending that kind of money anyway. You better get your father to buy you something like that."

"I was just joking."

"I know you was," said Ms. Jackie.

Todd looked over at the older model Range Rover parked in the grass. "I like that white Range Rover with the dark tint on the windows."

"You can have it for $7,000 down but the monthly bill will be $650," Mr. Jones Jr. said, looking down at his clipboard. "It's a 2007 model."

"I want it."

Mr. Jones Jr. looked over at Ms. Jackie, and she nodded her head. "Okay. Let me get started on the paperwork for you."

"Do you need me for anything else, Mr. Jones?" Ms. Jackie asked, adjusting her purse on her shoulder.

"Yes. I need you to fill out some forms and let me run a copy of your photo ID."

"Okay," Ms. Jackie said, and she followed him into the small, neatly decorated office enclosed in glass windows.

Todd walked over to the Range Rover. His smile spoke a thousand words. He peeked through the dark tint, but he was unable to see inside. He grabbed the door handle, and the door popped right open. The interior was peanut-butter-colored leather. There were JVC flat-screen TVs in the headrest and a JVC CD player in the console. The steering wheel looked to be made of red oak. There was also a built-in car alarm and an automatic start button by the ignition.

"They're really gonna hate on me now," he mumbled as he closed the door.

Close to 30 minutes later Ms. Jackie and Mr. Jones Jr. came out of the office with the paperwork.

"Love you, baby. I got to head off to the mall before it get too crowded. Everything's finished," Todd's mother said before she walked back to her chrome and black two-tone Harley Davidson F-150.

"I love you too, Mama. I'll see you later…and thanks!"

"Boy, don't be thanking me." She hopped in the truck and pulled off.

Mr. Jones Jr. handed Todd the automatic start device, ignition key, and all his necessary paperwork to drive the vehicle off the lot.

"Thank you, Mr. Jones."

Without another word, Mr. Jones Jr. smiled and walked back into the office.

Todd quickly pulled out his cell phone that was hanging from his waistband and called Hakim.

Hakim answered on the second ring. "What's the move, brah?" he asked with joy in his voice.

"Are you busy right now?"

"Not really. Why? What's up?"

"I just got a Range Rover from the Jones Dealership in College Park."

"For real? Nigga, you doing better than me."

Todd started laughing, noticing the sound of female voices in the background. "Who's all around you, shawty?"

"I'm at the house with Kee-Kee, Monica, and Cristal. They was just talking about what happened to you and Chris the other night."

"Yeah, that shit was crazy. But check this out...Bring Cristal with you to Jones Dealership so she can drive my dad's car back to his house."

"Okay. Hold on." Hakim set the phone down and yelled over his shoulder to Cristal, "Hey, girl, you wanna drive Money's car back to his house while Todd follow behind in his new Range Rover." After she answered, he talked back into the phone, "Hello?"

"Yeah, I'm here."

"She said she'll ride with me. We on the way, brah."

"Bet that," said Todd, and he hung up and jumped in his new Range Rover. He parked right next to the SS Monte Carlo, with the A/C booming.

Fifteen minutes later, Hakim was driving into the parking lot of the Jones Dealership with Cristal in the passenger seat, drinking iced tea.

Cristal stepped out of Hakim's Buick Regal. She was

dressed in a light green Louis Vuitton mini-dress, Louis Vuitton half-cut shirt that showed her flat stomach, and a pair of stilettos. Her shiny black hair was in a long ponytail, and her ebony eyes glowed as she looked around the parking lot for Todd.

Hakim remained in the car with the windows rolled up, enjoying the A/C.

Todd climbed out of his Range Rover. "You looking for me, my queen?"

Cristal turned to her right and saw Todd standing in front of his truck with his arms folded. "Hey, baby," she said, walking toward him like she was modeling for a fashion show. She smiled pleasantly as they embraced each other and shared a long, wet kiss on the mouth.

"How's your day going, my queen?"

"Great. Is this your new truck, baby?" she asked, running her hand along the smooth chrome rim.

"Yes it is!"

Hakim rolled the window down. "Let's get going, shawty. I got money to get."

Todd threw up his hands and handed Cristal the keys to the Monte Carlo. "Just follow me to my dad's house."

"Okay, baby."

Todd drove out of the parking lot slowly, and Cristal and Hakim followed behind.

* * *

When they got to Money's house, his Benz was gone, so Todd knew he wasn't there.

Cristal parked in front of the black gate that led to Money's swimming pool and gym that he'd had built right before Todd had graduated from high school.

She exited the Monte Carlo then jumped in the truck with Todd.

Todd pulled up beside Hakim and rolled the window down. "Thank you, brah. I'ma come by your house later."

"Okay. I like that Range Rover too, brah. You looking like a real businessman now."

Todd smiled.

"I gotta go get this money. Fuck with me later."

"You already know I will."

Hakim threw the peace sign up, the drove off.

Todd looked over at Cristal, who was looking in the mirror and putting on lip gloss. "Damn, you got some sexy-ass lips."

"I know, right? Just wait until I wrap them around your dick."

Todd unzipped his pants. "Let me see what you're talking about."

Cristal pulled his penis out and began licking up and down, until he came all in her mouth. She looked up at Todd as she swallowed every drop.

His eyes stretched wide with surprise. "Girl, you gonna make me fall in love with you."

"Boy, you late. I'm already in love with you."

"For real?"

"No. For fake," she teased, hitting him on the arm. "You know I love you, Todd. Stop playing."

Todd looked down at his watch and saw that it was 3:30 p.m. "Oh shit!"

"What's wrong?"

"I gotta drop you off right quick. I have business to

handle."

"Take me back to Kee-Kee's house then," Cristal said, rolling her eyes.

"Don't sound like that. I'll be back in no time, my queen. Give me that pretty smile to show me you love me."

She looked over at him and forced a tight smile.

Todd knew it was fake, but he had to go by the college and catch up with Beautiful, so he couldn't worry about Cristal at the moment. He wanted to know what all MT had been saying so he could be on point.

* * *

Todd's Range Rover rumbled to a stop in a cloud of dust as he pulled in front of Hakim's apartment.

Hollywood Court was a hot, dry, dusty set of apartments made of brown bricks. The city had been promising for years to fix the many potholes that lined the streets, but they hadn't fixed them yet.

Monica and Kee-Kee stood at the corner, smoking a blunt. They were both dressed in tan Polo shorts and white Polo halter tops that showed off their belly rings. They even had white Polo sandals to show off their fashionable, freshly polished pedicures. Their eyes locked on Todd's pearl-white Range Rover, and they tried to make out who was inside it.

"Girl, who is that? I never seen that truck out here before," Monica asked, trying to adjust her eyes to see through the darkly tinted windows.

"I don't know, but if it's the robbing crew, we need to get on the porch. I don't even have my gun on me."

Just as they started to walk off, the car door opened a

crack, then wider, and then Cristal stepped out.

"Aw, shit, girl! That's Cristal's ass," said Monica.

"Who she riding with?" Kee-Kee asked in a low tone that could only be heard by Monica.

"I don't know, but that mother-fucker is clean."

"Yeah, bitch! Next time, tell that nigga he better let us know who he is before I shoot that shit up."

"Aw, bitch, shut up. That's Todd in that truck," Cristal stated, stepping up on the porch.

"Damn!" they replied at the same time.

"Todd done came up on these ho-ass niggas around here," Kee-Kee said, passing Monica the blunt.

"He just bought it today," said Cristal.

"I should have stayed with his fine ass," Monica said, grinning from ear to ear.

Todd pulled off, honking his horn.

Cristal looked over at Monica with a serious face, and her ebony eyes seemed to darken.

"Damn, bitch! You looking like you wanna kill me. I was just joking with you. Chris is my boo."

"That's what's up. You had your chance years ago. Now it's mines."

Kee-Kee grabbed the handle of the screen door and smirked. "Both of y'all hoes shut up with that shit. Y'all blowing my high."

* * *

When Todd pulled into the S&T corner store, Beautiful, Peaches, and two of their groupies, their girlfriends, were standing in front of the payphone. Peaches and the two girls were talking to two light-skinned guys with red dreadlocks, while Beautiful stood alone, looking at her cell phone. It was clear that the guys were thugs because they wore their jeans hanging low, showing their boxers.

It was still sunny out but not too hot when Todd drove up to the payphone and hopped out of his Range Rover, poking his chest out proudly.

Beautiful was surprised when she saw who it was.

Peaches, the two girls, and the two thugs stopped conversing and stared Todd down like he was a celebrity or something.

Todd nodded his head at them, then walked up to Beautiful. "Can we talk for a minute?"

She already knew what he wanted to talk about because Peaches had confessed to telling him about MT's threats. Beautiful was really angry with Peaches for letting that cat out of the bag, but when MT called her phone around noon with threats of killing Todd, she realized the seriousness of it all. She knew then that Todd could get hurt. She lowered her head, then looked back up at Todd. "Yes, we can talk."

They both hopped into the truck, and everything was silent for a moment. Beautiful just stared out the passenger window at the ongoing traffic, and Todd stared at the dashboard, waiting for her to speak.

"So? What all did MT say to you? I want to know everything," he finally said.

She glanced over at him, grabbed his hand, and squeezed tightly. Tears began to stream down her face.

Todd leaned in and kissed her on the forehead. "It's going to be okay. Just let me know what he told you."

Her lips slowly parted. "He said he is going to kill you the next time he sees you," she said, covering her face with both hands.

Todd reclined in his seat and let his head fall against the headrest. "So this nigga want beef," he mumbled to himself.

Beautiful felt bad, realizing it was all because she didn't want to be with MT. "Maybe I can just make it work with him," she said.

Todd quickly cut his eyes over to her. "You don't have to do that. Fuck that pussy-ass nigga!" He gently grabbed her by the chin. "Now, you listen to me. Never let anyone make you do nothing you don't want to do. That shit he talking ain't nothing but talk. You are my woman now, and I got your back. Trust me!"

Todd's words brought comfort to all her worries and concerns. "You know all the right things to say to make me feel good. What am I going to do with you?"

He smiled, but the thought of MT saying he wanted to kill him wasn't sitting too well in his mind.

Beautiful wiped away her tears with the back of her hand, then leaned in and French kissed Todd in the mouth.

"I got to go handle some business, so call me later," said Todd.

"Okay. I will do that. Be careful."

"Oh, always!"

Beautiful climbed out of the truck, and Peaches ran up before she could close the door.

"Hey, Todd!" she said.

He grinned. "What's good, Peaches?"

"Tell my baby Hakim that I said to call me."

"I got you."

"Bye, baby," Beautiful said, then closed the door.

SCHOOL BOY

* * *

The room was quiet except for the sound of the piano keys striking their chords. Money Mac closed his eyes and allowed the spirit within to move him. As his fingers glided across the keys, he felt himself going down memory lane, to the time when his father had first shown him how to use a piano like a ho in the streets. He tried to hold back his feelings, but his mind kept flowing to all the wrong that had happened throughout his life. There was too much pain built up inside.

Money missed his best friend Mac-9 and wished he was free to enjoy the good life that he and Grip were enjoying. Even after twelve years, Mac-9 was still his right-hand man.

Money poured his innermost feelings out in front of a roomful of perfect strangers, not giving a damn if they appreciated it or not. His eyes began to water as he pressed down on the keys with the final note.

The audience erupted with applause. "Encore! Encore!" Even the band members were clapping.

Money stood up and took a bow. "Thank you," he said, inconspicuously wiping his eyes.

The short, Caucasian manager walked up to Money Mac and shook his hand. "That was a great performance, Mr. Jackson. The customers here say we need you here more often."

"I am very pleased to hear that, but this is not my profession, as you know. I just felt the need to come up here and play because it's been a while. This is one of my favorite restaurants in Atlanta, though, and I will forever eat here."

The manager grabbed the microphone in front of the piano. "Ladies and gentlemen, give Mr. Jackson another round of applause for his great performance!"

The crowd applauded again as Money walked back to his table.

"Now that's pimping," said Grip, enjoying his Cîroc.

Money reached over the table and gave Grip some dap. "Let's get out of here. That ho Sherri texted me about my money."

Grip downed the Cîroc. "Let's go then," he said, standing to his feet.

Rosay was one of Atlanta's classiest Jazz spots. Money and Grip often went there for some peace of mind. It was the first time Money had ever asked if he could play the piano.

Money and Grip waited on the sidewalk for the valet to pull up with the Mercedes-Benz. They were both dressed in custom Stacy Adams silk suits, with matching shoes and ties.

Within minutes, the valet was pulling into the lot and parked the Benz right in front of them.

* * *

In the car, Money called his ho Sherri and told her he'd be there to pick his money up within a half-hour.

Grip lit up a blunt while Al Green blasted through the speakers. It was half-past 8:00 in the evening when Money turned down Simpson Road to check up on his hoes who were working the block, selling their bodies.

Star, Sherri, and Misty strolled up and down the streets, looking for tricks who had money to spend. When they saw Money's Benz drive into the store parking lot, they walked over and pulled bankrolls of money out of their panties.

Money rolled down the window and reclined in his seat.

"Hey, Daddy. I made $3,000 so far," said Sherri, handing Money Mac his money.

"And what y'all hoes made today?"

Star and Misty stepped up to the window, smiling.

"I got $4,000, Daddy."

"And I only made $2,000, Daddy."

"Misty, ho, you need to tighten up. You too pretty to be only bringing $2,000 in."

"The next time you come through, Daddy, I'll have more. I'm just waiting on this trick who play for the Atlanta Falcons. He spend $1,000 or better when it come to me."

"Okay, my lady. Get back to work. I'll be back around 1:30 tonight."

They smiled at the same time, then walked off.

Money passed Grip the money to count as he pulled up at the red light. Money Mac glanced down at the CD player for only a second, but the sound of screeching rubber provoked his instincts and forced him to quickly look over his shoulder.

Three fully armed gunmen with ski masks covering their faces jumped out of a black Hummer H2, pointing M-16 machineguns directly at Money and Grip.

One of the gunmen walked over to the passenger door and demanded that Grip get out.

Money looked the gunman in the eyes as he slowly reached for his Smith & Wesson .45 under the seat.

"Get your bitch ass out of the car!" The gunman's voice was harsh and deep.

Grip looked over at Money as the gunman on his side grabbed the door handle.

"Fuck you, nigga!" Money yelled, raising his gun, but he was too slow.

A flashback of Todd being held in his arms as a baby came to his mind like a movie. He literally saw his life flash before his eyes as flying, screaming bullets cut through the Mercedes-Benz like a warm knife through butter. Gun smoke filled the air, and bullet shells sounded like chains falling from the sky. Grip's and Money Mac's bodies jerked violently, and women and kids who were walking around on the sidewalks ran for cover behind the parked cars along the curb. The scene looked like something out of The Godfather, when the don commanded his mobsters to carry out an assassination in the streets.

A young, slender, brown-skinned drug dealer, wearing a white wife-beater and jeans, peeked around the corner of an abandoned house just to see who was shooting. "Damn! That look like Money Mac's Benz!" His eyes zoomed in on the front tag that read M-O-N-E-Y, and the gold trim around the plate confirmed his suspicions.

The young dealer's name was C-Pain one of Money Mack's young protege's who he had schooled in the game at a young age. C-Pain was very well known around Atlanta as a young thug who got money but would kill on sight, without thinking twice. He had a lot of respect for Money and Grip because of the love they showed their 'hood. Besides that, Money was like a father to him.

C-Pain reached into both back pockets of his jeans and pulled out two silver Glock .40 handguns. He held the weapons up in a firing position, then ran from behind the house, right toward the gunmen like a madman on a mission.

Two bullets hit the gunman on the passenger side of Money's Benz, drilling right into his shoulder and causing his body to slam violently against the door.

The other two gunmen returned fire, giving their wounded partner enough time to hop in the Hummer.

C-Pain took cover behind a tree in the yard, while the gunmen all jumped in their truck and sped off. He quickly ran behind the Hummer, firing multiple shots, shattering the glass of the back windows. His adrenaline was rushing, and the sound of his heart beating at a tremendous rate was the only thing he could hear while he released those shots.

Kids cried at the top of their lungs out of fear, and car alarms sounded through the streets as C-Pain walked over to the Benz, still gripping his guns tightly. Money Mac lay in the driver seat, shaking, with thick black blood filling his mouth. C-Pain looked over at Grip, who was hanging halfway out of the car, dead, with his eyes wide open. "Someone call the fucking paramedics! This man is still alive!" C-Pain yelled to the people standing on their porches.

An old, slender black man came out of his house, leaning on a wooden cane. He had a phone in his other hand. "I called them, son. They're on the way," he said.

C-Pain got down on one knee and placed his guns on the ground. He grabbed Money by the hand. "Hang in there, Money. Warriors don't die from gunshot wounds. The paramedics are on their way."

The sounds of sirens came closer. C-Pain lightly patted Money on the leg, grabbed his guns off the ground, then took off running through the woods across the street.

Within minutes, Atlanta police, paramedics, crime scene investigators, and the Channel 2 news reporter Jeff Dore were there observing the scene, while yellow Crime Scene – Do Not Cross tape was placed all around Money's Benz.

* * *

Todd turned into Hollywood Court apartments, glancing at the neighborhood kids who were running around playing. The streetlights illuminated the car interior as Todd cruised up the dirt road and over the speed bump.

He had changed into jeans and a white wife-beater, but his face was still drawn because of the situation with MT.

Hakim, Chris, and a few younger hustlers from the 'hood were sitting on the hood of Hakim's Buick Regal, drinking beer and smoking weed.

Todd parked his Range Rover on the basketball court right across from Hakim's apartment because he didn't want to leave it out in the dusty road.

Chris and Hakim strolled over to the court to examine Todd's new truck.

"There he is, the one and only big-baller," Hakim said, walking up to Todd and giving him some dap.

Todd smiled.

Chris embraced him and offered a friendly handshake, then whispered in his ear, "We will be seeing some good money in a few days. I am just waiting on this Mexican in Gainesville to get back with me."

"Brah, I know you gonna handle business. That's why I fuck with you. Me, you, and Hakim going to take over this shit."

"What I miss?" Hakim said, jumping into the conversation. "I heard you say my name."

"I was just tellin' Chris me, you, and him is going to take over the West Side."

"And how we gon' do that?"

"My dad gave me two kilos of pure cocaine."

"Oh, hell yeah! That's a big start for us. Money told me to get at him anyway. I'll call him later, because I know him and Grip somewhere getting to the money."

"After I cook the two bricks, it will bounce back double, so we looking at doubling each brick."

"Shawty, that's what's up. We can take off with that much money," said Todd.

"Do you already have any sales?"

"Hell yeah! I was just telling Todd that I got some Mexicans I fuck with up in Gainesville, spending good money."

Todd spotted Jay-Bo's Mercedes-Benz ML63 coming up the street with all four windows rolled down and the music beating loud. "Hold up a minute, shawty," Todd replied, walking to the dirt road, waving Jay-Bo down to stop.

When Jay-Bo saw Todd, he pulled over and stopped. "What's good, young Todd? Why didn't you call me?"

"I had a lot of shit going on all day. Your boy MT sending word around, saying that he wants to do me in."

"What? Hold on. Let me call this nigga." Jay-Bo grabbed his cell phone off the passenger seat and dialed MT number, but the phone only rang and went to voicemail. "His ass ain't picking up right now. Don't worry about him, young gangster. He work for me. Get in so I can get you that gun Money wanted you to have."

"Yeah." Todd turned around to Hakim and Chris, who were looking around in his Range Rover. "Say, bro, I'ma ride with Jay-Bo for a minute. Watch the truck until I get back."

"I got you, bro!" Hakim yelled, wiping his fingers across the soft leather interior.

Todd hopped in the car with Jay-Bo, and they pulled off.

After kicking it with Hakim for a few more minutes Chris headed out.

* * *

Less than thirty minutes later, Jay-Bo and Todd were pulling into the garage of a huge green and white house that sat on a hill. The front porch was made of white bricks, and the grass was neatly trimmed with a few flowers that circled around a large pine tree.

As soon as Jay-Bo parked, an older, gray-headed man with a 9mm tucked in his waistband came walking out the side door.

"What's good, Unc?" Jay-Bo asked.

"Nothing much, nephew. Just coming out to check up on you."

Jay-Bo and Todd climbed out of the Benz. "Unc," Jay-Bo said, "this is Money's son Todd. Todd, this is my Uncle Jacob."

Jacob walked over to Todd and shook his hand. "What's good, young blood? I know you're a boss if you're Money Mac's son."

Todd smiled, looking around at the power tools that hung on the walls. "Yeah. I'm in college."

"Well, you got the right mindset, because being out here in these streets only leads to two things—graveyard or prison for life."

"Come on, Todd. Follow me downstairs to the basement."

They walked through the living room, where two young thugs with dreads were posted at the front windows, with AK-47 rifles in their hands. Jay-Bo used them as lookout men. If anyone ever tried to creep up and rob the trap house, those two would open fire without questioning.

They made their way down the stairs and into the basement. When Jay-Bo pulled the steel door open, Todd was surprised to see the many guns, hunting knives, and bulletproof vests that lined the walls.

"I already see the one I want," said Todd.

"Oh yeah? Which one?"

Todd walked over to the wall and grabbed two twin Glock .45 handguns. They were small enough to fit right in the palm of his hand. "I want these two bitches right here."

Jay-Bo smiled, leaning against the wall with his arms folded.

* * *

"I'm leaving for a minute, Kee-Kee!" Hakim yelled from the kitchen as he grabbed his .45 off the counter.

"Come in the living room for a minute, babe," she shouted over the hum of the hairdryer.

Hakim walked in the living room to see what Kee-Kee wanted. Her eyes were glued to the TV screen. "What you want, girl?" he asked.

"Someone just got killed on Simpson Road today. Turn the TV up right quick."

Hakim placed his gun on the sofa and grabbed the remote control off the glass table. "Girl, turn that damn hairdryer off!"

She obliged his command.

There was a reporter broadcasting for a minute, and then the screen cut to an aerial view from a helicopter.

Kee-Kee's and Hakim's eyes grew big when the reporter announced Money's and Grip's real names.

Kee-Kee grabbed her purse off the floor and fumbled around for her cell phone. With her heart thumping, she punched in Todd's number on the speed dial. "C'mon...c'mon!" Her fingers barely complied; her hands were shaking. As she waited for the call to connect, Hakim's phone began to ring.

"You calling Todd?" Hakim asked, walking back and forth like he was about to lose his mind.

She nodded. "C'mon, Todd," she pleaded, almost silently, watching Money's Benz being lifted onto a flatbed truck. When Todd's voicemail picked up, she said, "Todd, this is me, Kee-Kee. When you get to your phone, call me ASAP."

"Let me see that phone." Hakim quickly snatched the phone out of her hand and dialed Money's number. It also went straight to voicemail. He then called Ms. Jackie's number, and she picked up on the third ring, crying. "Have you sent he news, Mama?" Hakim asked.

"He's dead, Hakim! Where's my baby?"

"Kee-Kee just tried to call him, but he ain't picking up. His truck is over here, so he should be back in a few," he said, holding back tears.

"I called him too. Oh God! I hope my son is okay."

"He is, Mama. Just calm down."

The news reporter came back to the screen, reporting that Money Mac was still alive but in critical condition with multiple shots to the chest.

"Mama, the news reporter just said Money's still alive!"

"I'm on my way to Grady Hospital."

"We'll be down there when Todd gets here."

"Okay. Bye." And with that, she hung up.

SCHOOL BOY

* * *

Within minutes, word spread throughout Hollywood Court that Money and Grip had been shot. Hakim had called up Chris and Monica, while Kee-Kee called Cristal. Still, there was no sign of Todd, even after an hour had passed.

The young drug dealer in Hollywood Court Apartments hopped in their cars, fully armed and looking for the ones who'd dared to fire on Money and Grip. Everyone thought it had to be a robbery, because Money and Grip had no enemies that anyone knew of—especially since they supplied nearly half the city with cocaine fresh off the ship.

When Jay-Bo and Todd pulled into Hollywood Court, people were murmuring all around.

"What in the fuck they got going on out there?" Todd asked.

"Shit, I don't know, but whatever it is, it's serious."

Hakim spotted Jay-Bo's Benz and ran to it. "Boy, why you ain't been answering your phone?"

Todd looked down at his cell phone that was clipped to one side of his belt. His ringer was on silent, and there were thirty-three missed calls. "My shit was on silent. How in the fuck did this happen?" Todd asked, glancing up at Hakim.

"What's up with all these people out tonight?"

Hakim looked at Todd closely. "It's…Money."

"What about Money? Shawty, come out with it."

"He got shot…and Grip is dead."

Todd and Jay-Bo started laughing.

"Shawty, go 'head on with that bullshit," Todd said, but then he realized Hakim wasn't smiling at all. "Wait…you're serious?"

"Damn right! It's all over the news."

Jay-Bo's phone rang. "Hello?"

"Brah, Money and Grip just got shot up on Simpson," GG said from the other end. "I got C-Pain right here with me. He said three niggas in a black Hummer shot them. I'm on my way to Grady Hospital, because he said Money was still alive when he left."

"Okay. I'll be down in a few minutes. I got Todd and Hakim right here with me."

"Tell shawty we will get to the bottom of this."

"Check that," Jay-Bo said and ended the call. He turned to Todd. "That was GG. He's on his way down to Grady, because C-Pain say he saw the whole thing, and Money was still alive."

Tears began to fall from Todd's eyes as he reached in the back seat and grabbed the twin Glocks and bulletproof vest. Without saying a word, he hopped out of the car and ran for his truck. Hakim and Jay-Bo yelled for him, but Todd just looked back and told them he was on his way to Grady Hospital.

"Hey, brah, you, Kee-Kee, Monica, and Cristal meet us there," Hakim said, tossing his car keys to Chris before he jumped in the truck with Todd.

* * *

Grady Hospital was an architect's dream. It stood ten stories high, with huge glass windows, marble floors in the lobby, and a small gift shop that sold flowers, balloons, and teddy bears, and freshly painted pure white walls. The ceiling was made of glass, and the air was fresh and cold.

Todd pulled into the parking lot across from McDonald's and parked. He and Hakim quickly jumped out of the truck and ran toward the front desk.

A very pretty, light-skinned lady who looked to be in her late twenties was sitting in a chair, with her eyes buried in an issue of Success Magazine.

Todd hit the counter with his fist. "Do you have a patient by the name of Jackson?"

She quickly raised her head and frowned. "First of all, don't be hitting my desk like that," she said with attitude.

Todd bit down on his lip, balling up his fists.

Hakim grabbed him by the shoulder. "Calm down, shawty. Let me handle her before she calls security."

"Yeah, you do that, before I slap the bitch!"

"Excuse me, Ms. Lady, but my best friend's father just got shot. We are only trying to find out what floor he's on."

"I'm sorry to hear that, but he needs to remain calm," she said, looking through the patient book. "You say his name is Jackson?"

"Yes."

"He's in the operating room on the fourth floor."

"Okay. Thank you, beautiful."

When Todd and Hakim stepped off the elevator, they saw Ms. Jackie sitting in the waiting room, with her head leaning against the wall.

"Mama! You okay?" Todd asked, standing in the threshold of the waiting room door.

"Oh, hey, baby. Yes, I'm okay. Are you okay?"

"Yes. What are they saying about Dad?"

"He's still in the operating room, babe."

Less than ten minutes later, Kee-Kee, Monica, Chris, and

Cristal came rushing into the waiting room, talking loudly.

Ms. Jackie stood up and walked into the hallway.

Todd sat alone in the corner, thinking over what little information he'd been given about his father being in the emergency room.

Jay-Bo, GG, and C-pain stepped in, and C-Pain walked over to Todd and knelt down. "What's good, Todd? I'm C-Pain."

They shook hands.

"Me and your dad are good friends. I seen the whole thing."

Todd gave him a look that said he wasn't trying to talk.

C-Pain felt the vibe, but he also knew what Todd was going through, so he took a seat in the chairs next to the window.

An hour had passed, and everyone sat patiently waiting on the doctor to give them an up-to-date report on Money Mac's condition.

All of the sudden, the emergency room doors slid open, and a short Hispanic doctor in his mid-thirties came out, pulling off a set of latex gloves. He walked up to Ms. Jackie with his hand extended. The look on his face was completely serious. "Ms. Ellis, I don't know how to say this, but…well, we lost him," the doctor announced. "I'm sorry. We did everything we could."

Todd stepped in front of his mother with tears streaming down his face. "What the fuck you mean y'all lost him? Get out of my way!" He pushed the doctor to the side and walked through the emergency room door. Even when the doctor yelled for him to stop, he kept going.

Three doctors with blue masks on their mouths stood over Money Mac's body, stretched across the operating table.

Blood was everywhere. Todd stood at the door with a shocked look on his face. There, dead on that table, was the man who had shown him everything there was to know in life.

One of the surgeons noticed Todd standing at the door. "You can't be in here!" he yelled.

Todd took off running down the hallway with the feeling of hate engulfing his heart.

* * *

When the elevator opened, two black men in dark blue business suits stepped off. Ms. Jackie immediately knew they were detectives because of the badges that hung over their waistbands.

"Hi there, are you Ms.Ellis?"

"Yes I am."

Ms. Ellis. I'm Detective Poe from Homicide, and this is my partner, Detective Hill," the tall, bald-headed detective introduced, looking down at a picture of Todd, Ms. Jackie, and Money Mac.

"Well, it's nice to meet you two, but unfortunately, I don't have any information on who killed my son's father."

"I know it's very hard for you right now, but when you do think of anything, please call us at this number." He reached into his coat pocket and handed her a small card.

"When I hear anything, I will contact your office."

They both nodded, then walked into the operating room to examine Money's body.

CHAPTER 10

It was June 17, 2012. Just as the casket was being lowered into the ground, the clouds darkened, and rain began to fall. It seemed so appropriate, like even Mother Nature was grieving Money's loss.

Ms. Jackie grasped the hand of Todd tightly and began to cry.

Todd stared down into the six-foot-deep hole with a frown on his face. For the past three days, he'd been staying at his father's house, crying until he couldn't cry anymore. All he could think about was getting revenge for the deaths of Money and Grip.

Hakim, Chris, and a few pimps from Memphis, Tennessee stood across from Money's three prostitutes, Sherri, Star, and Misty.

Detectives Poe and Hill stood under a tree, watching the many drug dealers who'd come to pay their respects.

Grip's family had his body transferred to Daytona Beach, Florida, where he was originally from.

"I can't believe he's gone! I just can't believe it!" Ms. Jackie cried out.

"It's gonna be all right, Mama."

After the minister said a few last words, Todd exchanged emotional hugs with friends and family, then escorted his mother over to where his best friend, Hakim, was standing.

"Are you okay, Todd?" Hakim asked.

"I'll be fine. I just need a minute alone. Can you take Mama to the limo and wait for me?"

"No problem."

Todd handed over his umbrella and told his mother to go with Hakim to the car.

She smiled and gave him a gentle kiss on the cheek. "I understand, baby. Take all the time you need."

The rain began to come down even harder as Todd knelt at the edge of the grave. He turned his head toward the sky and reached his hands out, as if to confirm that the rain was real. He wanted to break down and cry, but he fought it. That was as close as he was ever going to be to his father again, and he wanted to spend those last moments talking the way they used to. Todd had unresolved issues and needed to release. Deep down in his heart, he knew his father could hear him. "Dad, I've always admired you for being so strong and providing for me and Ma. I never wanted for anything—not money, not attention, and definitely not love. But despite how great you were as a father, I hope and pray that God allowed you a chance to enter the gates of Heaven. I promise you, I will find the mother-fucker who did this to you, even if it takes me putting my life on the line."

His voice choked up, and tears began to well up in his eyes. He quickly leaned his head back and allowed the rain to wash them away. He took a deep breath and continued, "Now, don't start with your preaching. I'm not some cheap prostitute hanging out on street corners. Thank you for all you have shown me. I won't let you down. Rest in peace, Dad. Oh yeah…I forgot. Tell Grip pimping ain't dead. Those niggas just scared. I love you, Dad!"

That said, Todd burst out laughing, hoping to find comfort. He stood up and brushed the mud off his pants, then pulled a neatly folded piece of paper out of his suit pocket. On it was a song he'd written especially for his father, entitled, "When Players Enter the Kingdom of Heaven." He kissed it and threw it on top of the casket. "I played this song for you on the piano at church earlier." He smiled. "I know you'll like it. Everyone else did. Well, let me get going before I get sick in this rain."

As Todd walked toward his truck, he glanced over at the two detectives and smiled.

CHAPTER 11

It had been two weeks since the murders of Money Mac and Grip, and still Todd hadn't found out who'd killed them. He climbed out of the king-sized bed, looking a mess. He wasn't exactly keeping up his appearance because he had bigger things on his mind. He had grown a full beard and hadn't had his hair braided in two weeks. Todd had isolated himself from the world and was living at his mother's crib, where he felt safe and loved.

From time to time, he called Cristal and Beautiful just to check up on them. He even called Chris and Hakim to let them know they could keep all the money from the kilos Money had given him. They both rejected Todd's generous offer and gave him $40,000 in cash.

In his Will, Money Mac had left Todd three cars, the mini-mansion, and half a million dollars, though he wouldn't get it till he graduated from college with his business degree. Todd decided to sell the mansion and cars because they brought back too many memories.

He walked over to the mirror that hung on the closet door and observed himself. When took a good look at his reflection, he realized how bad he really looked. "Damn! I gotta get this shit off my face," he said to himself, gently rubbing his face.

He knew it had to be midmorning because the sun was beaming through all the windows. He figured it was a good day to go by Money's house and clean up a little.

After Todd shaved, he took a quick shower and got dressed in his wife-beater, a pair of jeans, his white Air Force 1 shoes, and an Atlanta fitted cap. He peeked into his mother's room just to tell her he was heading out, but she was gone.

Todd grabbed a piece of paper from the top shelf in the living room and wrote a note for her:

Dear Mama,

I went by Money's crib to clean up a little. I'll be back around 10:00 p.m. Don't wait up for me. Love you!

Your son,

Todd

He then placed the note on the kitchen counter for her to find.

Todd headed for the garage. Over the sound of the automatic door lifting up, Money's pit bull, Princess, started barking. He rubbed the dog on the top of her head, then hopped in his Range Rover.

* * *

Within forty-five minutes, Todd was pulling into the driveway of Money's luxury mini-mansion. He parked behind the gray Aston-Martin, gold Range Rover Sport truck, and SS Monte Carlo that Money Mac had left behind.

As he entered the beautiful landscaped yard, he could hear the radio playing. When he got up to the porch, the radio went off. Todd pecked through the window and saw no one, so he decided to walk around the back, just to get a better look.

Just as he stepped off the porch, the front door flew open. "Oh! Todd!" a soft voice greeted.

He turned around, only to find the housekeeper standing in the door, with two black trash bags in her hands. "Hey there, Destiny. What made you stop by? I mean, my dad has been dead for two weeks now."

"I just couldn't keep staying at home with nothing to do. I've been working for your father for nearly three years. This is my life." She pointed at the trash in the bags.

"I understand, but did you know I'm selling the house and cars?"

"Nope. Why would you do that? Your dad put his life into having this place built from the ground up. This place was part of all the hard work he put into it."

"Look, Destiny, I understand all that, but how in the hell am I supposed to keep up with a mortgage payment? My dad had money. Me? I'm just Todd without a dad."

She set the bags down. "You are somebody. When I see you, I see Money Mac all over again. Yes, I'm just a housekeeper, but your father showed me more love than my own father. He gave you something no one can take away."

"And what's that?"

She smiled. "Knowledge on how to come up in this world. Money is dead, but his knowledge lives within you, his son." She picked up the bags and walked off.

Todd stood at the bottom of the stairs, pondering what Destiny had said. He knew she was right and on point with all his father had taught him. Damn, she's right! But before I do anything, I gotta find my father's killer, he thought, then walked through the door and closed it behind him.

The first place Todd went was to the safe Money had

hidden behind the picture of him and Jackie on the wall. Back when he was just a kid, Money had installed that safe for him in case of any emergency. Todd had vowed never to open it until he really needed to.

The digital combination code was his birthday. When he pressed the confirm button, the steel door slowly opened. Inside, he found $80,000 in cash, seven kilos of pure cocaine, four pounds of neatly wrapped marijuana, and a black Smith & Wesson .45 handgun.

Todd smiled, then grabbed his cell phone from his waistband. He punched in Hakim's number on the speed dial. When Hakim answered on the second ring, with joy in his voice, Todd told him about the seven kilos of cocaine.

Hakim agreed to help sell them. Hakim also informed Todd that he'd kept a close tab on the mess going on in the city and that he'd gotten word on about who might have had something to do with Money and Grip being killed.

Todd told Hakim to meet him at his mother's house around midnight so they could discuss the information Hakim had gathered in the streets.

After Todd hung up with Hakim, he grabbed everything from the safe, placed it in a large trash bag, then walked out the front door.

Something was weighing heavily on Todd's mind as he hopped into his truck. Most of it had to do with the thought of finding out who had killed his father.

The sound of a helicopter flying above in the sky made him so nervous that he began to scan his surroundings with his eyes. As soon as he saw that everything was safe, he sped out of the driveway, glancing every so often in the rearview mirror.

* * *

Thirty-five minutes later, Todd was pulling into the BP gas station on Simpson Road. Before getting out, he looked over at the young hustlers standing in front of the Chinese store serving fiends. He looked to his right and spotted Hakim and Chris talking to two beautiful girls getting out of a red Enzo Ferrari. Todd pulled up beside the Ferrari and jumped out.

"What the business is, shawty?" Hakim asked when he saw Todd step out of his truck.

Todd gave Hakim and Chris some dap. "Nothing much on my end. I was coming over here to get some gas, then I saw y'all posted up with these two sexy ladies."

The two women began to blush.

"But on the real though, I need to discuss serious business with y'all."

"That's what's up! Hey, Tasha and Kierra, y'all got the cell phone number. Hit me later," said Hakim.

"Okay," Kierra responded before she walked into BP.

"Shawty, pull my truck up at Pump 3 while I pay for this gas."

Chris did as he was told.

Todd and Hakim strolled into BP, paid for the gas, then went back to the truck. The hopped into Todd's Range Rover, and he reached in the back seat and grabbed the black trash bag.

Chris finished pumping the gas then sat in the back seat, looking puzzled.

Todd handed Hakim the bag. "Check out what's inside."

Hakim reached into the trash bag and pulled out one brick of pure cocaine. When Chris saw what it was, his eyes lit up like shiny diamonds.

"This is our chance to come up. My dad left me this shit, so we are taking over the city."

Hakim nodded his head, and a smile came over his face.

"Let me see that, shawty," said Chris, leaning over the passenger seat.

"Anybody who gets in our way gets it. All fun and games are over. Fuck the bullshit." Hakim cut his eyes over at Todd. "So, you ready to take on the real world?"

"Ready? My dad is dead, shawty. I can't just sit back and allow the niggas who killed my father the chance of enjoying that pleasure."

Chris and Hakim remained silent as Todd spoke from the heart.

"Now that I'm speaking on this, what's the word on who did it? Who killed my dad?"

"First, let's get off this hot-ass Simpson with all this dope on us," Hakim replied.

Todd slowly pulled out of the gas station.

"The word on the street is that MT had something to do with those murders. My peoples say the hit was meant for you. He knew you'd been ridin' around in the Benz, and it just so happened that Money and Grip were in the car that day."

"How good is your people's word?"

"Platinum, baby."

As Todd stopped at the red light, he started beating on the steering wheel. "I'ma kill that fuck nigga, shawty!"

"Brah, calm down! An angry man can't think. We will get his ass, but we plan first. It's not your fault shit went the way it did. The good thing is, me and Chris didn't lose our only brother."

Todd looked at Hakim, then at Chris, then smiled. "This nigga wants war? Well, now he's got one!"

Chris reached over Hakim's shoulder and handed him a blunt filled with marijuana.

Hakim lit it up. "Here, brah. Calm your nerves with this good shit."

"I need this for real. Brah, you can ride the other Range Rover over at the house. The keys will be at my mother's house."

"Check that, boss man."

Todd liked the sound of those words, "boss man." He smiled as he exhaled the smoke through his nose.

Twenty minutes later, he was dropping Hakim and Chris off in Hollywood Court Apartments with seven kilos of cocaine and four pounds of weed. He kept the money and gun in his possession.

Todd drove back to the mansion his father had left him, hoping to find some peace of mind.

CHAPTER 12

Hakim and Chris were feeling like a million bucks as they pulled into Pin-Ups Strip Club, listening to "16 Fever" by Gucci Mane.

It was the Fourth of July, and the weather was gorgeous. The line wrapped around the corner, and valet parking was full.

Todd pulled up in his gray Aston Martin, blowing the horn and flashing the headlights three times. The valet stepped aside, and the bright orange partitions parted like the Red Sea.

For the past week, money had been coming in good for Hakim, Chris, and Todd. Todd even decided to move off the college campus and into the mini-mansion his father had left to him.

The stocky, bald-headed valet leaned over in Todd's window. "Are those guys in that gold Range Rover with you?"

"Yeah. Let them in too, so they can park."

"See? I still remember the signal."

"I like that, um…what's your name again?"

"Ali, like the boxer."

Todd handed Ali a $100 tip, just like he always did when Ali let him through. "Thanks for the hook-up."

"Anytime!"

Hakim followed behind Todd as they parked in the back lot, where all the big-time ballers parked. Todd made sure his bulletproof vest was strapped on tight under his Polo shirt, then reached under the seat and grabbed his twin Glock .45s. Every since he'd found out that MT had put a hit out on him, he made sure to wear the vest Jay-Bo had given him.

Todd never mentioned to Jay-Bo or GG about the information he'd received from Hakim, as he didn't want to put MT on point. He felt that the less Jay-Bo knew, the better his chances were of catching MT slipping when the time was right. It wasn't that Todd didn't trust Jay-Bo or GG; he just knew MT was bringing in good money for them and they would want to ask questions first.

Todd placed his pistols in the glove compartment, then got out of the car and looked around the parking lot. One thing his father had always taught him was to never get too comfortable with his surroundings. Although the club was in the affluent east Atlanta section, he knew anything could happen at any time.

Hakim, Chris, and Todd walked slowly toward the glass door that led to the VIP section. The security guard was a stocky, bald man with arms the size of cannons and an attitude Todd could read from twenty paces. Todd reached into his front pants pocket and handed the security guard a $50 bill.

The guard's expression immediately formed into a smile. He then stepped to the side and allowed them to walk in.

The room was crowded, and the lights were dim. Todd, Hakim, and Chris sat at the table in the VIP section, which was situated across from the stage and consisted of six tables and two booths. Some people perceived it as a place of status, but for Todd, it was a comfortable seat away from the petty ballers yelling like fools.

The DJ played the song "In Love with a Stripper" by T-Pain, while the guys standing around the stage stuffed dollar bills into the strippers' thongs.

When three beautiful women wearing high heels and thongs made their way through the crowd and into the VIP section, Hakim looked back at the short security guard and held up two fingers. The security guard walked into a small room and came back two minutes later with two stacks of dollar bills, wrapped in plastic. Hakim grabbed the money, gave one stack to Todd, and split the other stack with Chris.

All three strippers had the body of Buffy and the face of a beautiful model. The one standing in front of Todd leaned in and whispered something in his ear. She then started rotating her body like a snake, gently caressing her hips. The other two strippers danced in front of Hakim and Chris as they threw dollar bills at their feet.

The crowd erupted. Red, green, and orange lights flashed in rhythm to the music. Todd, Hakim, and Chris were having the time of their lives, popping a bottle of Cristal and throwing money in the air, makin' it rain like Li'l Wayne says.

Hakim got up to go to the restroom, and he spotted MT and a few of his friends walking toward the exit door. He immediately tapped Todd on the shoulder. "Shawty, that's that nigga MT right there, leaving out the door."

Todd quickly jumped to his feet, looking over the crowd at MT as he walked out the front door. "Let's go! I want that nigga now."

Without saying another word, Hakim and Chris followed behind Todd like they were his bodyguards. When they got to the parking lot, MT was pulling off in his Dodge Viper.

Todd noticed one of the MT's friends walking to a car across the street, next to the dark and creepy alley. "That's one of his homeboys. Let's follow him!"

Hakim and Chris jumped in his Range Rover, and Todd in the Aston as they sped out of the lot behind MT's friend.

After about forty-five minutes, he pulled up at a green and white house. All the lights in the house were off, and an old sofa sat on the front porch. The guy was grabbing something out of the trunk of his car when Todd crept up behind him. Seconds later the man was out cold from the impact of Todd's heavy blow from the butt of his gun.

* * *

Todd, Hakim, and Chris stood there looking at the man who was duct taped to the wooden chair. The room was tiny and airless. There were no windows and no paintings on the walls to stare at. A small heat light hung from the ceiling.

Hakim grabbed the bucket off the floor and poured whatever was in it into the man's face.

The captive looked resigned as he opened his eyes. He then murmured a few words. The man wakened to Hakim standing over him playing with a lighter. He then picked up on a distinctive smell in the air. Lighter fluid! Hakim had dumped it all over him, and he was soaked with it. "No! Don't do this! I-I have kids," he screamed when Todd removed the tape from his mouth.

"That's good you have kids. This won't be long at all because you will answer all of my questions."

The man nodded in agreement.

"Okay. First question, who are you and what do you know

about two guys being shot to death on Simpson a few weeks ago?"

"My name is Grady Parker. I'm twenty-eight years old and, brah, I don't even be on Simpson."

Todd backhanded him in the mouth. "Bitch! Did I say you be on Simpson?"

Tears began to fall from his eyes as he nodded.

"Who are you to MT?"

"That's my first cousin. Brah, I didn't know he was going to kill old boy. I was just with him."

Todd looked at Hakim, then Chris. "It's okay, Grady. Now, this question will determine if you live or die. What would you do if someone killed your father if he was all you had?"

"To be real, I would probably kill them."

"Good answer." Todd tossed the lighter into Grady's lap, and the flame ignited the liquid, instantly burning through his clothes. A deathening scream came from the man's throat as he sat there helplessly, watching the flames light up his body. His arms jerked up, and his toes and feet curled in like a baby's. There were unbearable rips of pain as his flesh cooked to the seat.

Hakim, Todd, and Chris watched as Grady yelled.

Todd himself began to smile. He had never thought seeking revenge could have felt so good. "Hakim, find out where MT lay his head."

"Okay. I'm on it," Hakim said, whipping out his cell phone and calling his partner, T-Man, who lived in Decatur.

T-Man was one of Hakim's main customers in the drug business. Whenever he wanted some work from Hakim, he would buy two or three kilos at a time. Whenever Hakim wanted some information about what was going on in the streets, T-Man was the man to call. T-Man knew everything that was going on throughout the city of Atlanta, from the major drug deals to the many murders that took place. No one ever knew where he got his information from, but if he said it, nine times out of ten, he was right.

When Hakim's phone call went straight to voicemail, he left a message for T-Man to get back with him ASAP.

All the men exited the house and went their own way, promising to meet back up tomorrow.

* * *

The streets were silent, and the moon was full. Todd drove through downtown Atlanta with all four windows rolled down. The speedometer on his Aston-Martin barely reached twenty-five. He passed the Five-Point Train Station, thinking about the first time he and his father had gone to the Underground across the street. At Burgess', he stopped in the middle of the empty street, debating whether or not to drive on. Money Mac's death was heavy on his mind and he really didn't know what to do or where to go at this point.

All of the sudden, his phone rang. He looked at the screen, he answered. It was Beautiful. "What's good, baby girl?"

"Lying here in bed, thinking about you."

"Oh? Is that right?"

"I want you to come pick me up."

Todd looked through his rearview mirror and noticed a car pulling up behind him. "Hold on a second, Beautiful." He placed the phone on his lip, grabbed his pistol from the passenger seat, then drove off slowly. When he saw the car turning onto another street, he felt relieved. "Hello? You still there?"

"Yes, I'm here, baby," she said softly.

"I will be there to pick you up shortly. Just be standing out front, because I don't want to hear that fake-ass security guard bitching."

"Okay. I'll be waiting in my hallway until I see you pull up."

"I'm driving my gray Aston-Martin."

"You done came up, I see."

"Yeah. My dad left me this car. Wait till you see my house."

"Okay then. I am excited, boo. I'll see you in a few."

"Check that."

He hung up and called Hakim to let him know that he would be with Beautiful for the remainder of the night, but it went straight through to voicemail. Hakim and Chris were planning to stop by the mansion after they were finished handling some late night business with the Mexican's in Gainesville, but Todd didn't want any interruption while Beautiful was over, so he left a message.

* * *

Thirty minutes later, Todd was pulling into Clark Atlanta college parking lot, before he came to a stop, Beautiful ran out of the hallway of her dormitory with a bag of clothes in her hand.

Todd quickly stopped when he saw her approaching the passenger door.

She hopped in, wearing shorts that showed her thighs and

a shirt that revealed her stomach. Her hair was pulled back in a ponytail, and her DD breasts stood up like two cannon balls. Her thick calves and small waist had Todd's eyes locked on her.

She leaned over and kissed his lips. "Damn, boy. I missed you."

"I missed you too, with them sexy legs."

She smiled and gave him an innocent look. "Baby, this is a nice-ass car."

"I know, right? Hell, I don't even drive my Range Rover like I used to," he said, pulling out of the parking lot.

"So…how have you been holding up? I haven't seen you around in a couple of days."

"I've been really busy, trying to get things back how they once was when my dad was living."

"Oh. Okay."

"I talked to my teacher. He said I will still be given credit because he knows how it is to lose a father. But enough about me. What's been going on with you? Has old boy called you lately?"

"Who? MT?"

"Uh-huh." His voice was as casual as a spring day.

"Hell naw! And he better not either."

They conversed until Todd pulled into his driveway. Beautiful was amazed when she saw the mini-mansion he was living in.

As they got out of the car, Todd opened his mouth to say something, but Beautiful put her finger over his lips. She smiled at him, took him by the hand, and pulled him toward the neatly trimmed grass.

"Hold on, baby girl. Let's take this in the house."

"Okay, Daddy."

After deactivating the house alarm system, he unlocked the deadbolt so they could go inside. "Make yourself at home while I go to the back for a minute. There's food in the refrigerator, and there's a bar if you want anything to drink."

"Okay." She glanced over at the twenty-foot-long aquarium that was built into the wall, filled with an assortment of tropical fish.

Todd quickly took off his bulletproof vest and laid his twin Glocks on the bed. He reached under the king-sized bed and pulled out a black leather briefcase. Inside were ten stacks of $100 bills that Hakim and Chris had made for him over the weekend. When he saw that all the money was still in place, he closed the briefcase and hit it in the walk-in closet behind his shoes.

When he walked back out to the living room, he noticed Beautiful sipping on a glass of vodka, glancing around the room at the pictures of Money Mac that were still hung on the wall. Todd's footsteps on the floor startled her, and she quickly turned around, holding her chest. "You frightened me!"

"Sorry. Didn't mean to. So, do you like the place?"

"Like it? Daddy, I love this place! Is that real money embedded in the floor?"

"Nah. My father had that custom made."

"He was rich, I see."

Todd laughed. "Well, you could say that."

"You mind if I look around?"

"Be my guest."

She walked over to the large, shiny, black grand piano and pressed the keys. "Can you play this?"

"What, the piano? Sure."

"Play something for me."

"Okay." Todd walked over to the piano and sat down on the stool. He played the same song he'd played at his father's funeral.

Beautiful was hypnotized, in love, and really horny as she stared into his eyes. She set her glass on top of the piano, walked over to Todd, and French kissed him. He ran his fingers across her ass as she reached in his pants and began to slowly stroke his penis back and forth. Todd undid her zipper and lowered her shorts down around her ankles. He then began gently running his finger in and out of her wetness. He stood up, undid his belt, and opened his zipper. Beautiful helped him take off his shirt and pants, then threw them on the floor. The only thing Todd was still wearing was a pair of boxers and his shoes. She got down on her knees and took the tip of his manhood in her mouth and sucked on it. He moaned as his salty pre-cum drizzled out onto her tongue. She then took the head out of her mouth and ran the tip of her tongue up and down the middle of his shaft, which made him moan even louder. All of Todd's worries were gone, and he felt like he was in Heaven.

"Hold on. Let me show you something," Todd said as he lifted her up and sat her on top of the piano. He opened her legs, then slowly ran his tongue up and down her clit, until she lay back and began moaning loudly.

She got down from the piano and bent over the stool. Todd slowly eased his penis into her wetness as she ground her hips into him. He filled her up good, and after a few more strokes, Todd came inside of her.

Still, that wasn't good enough for Beautiful, so she started giving him hand action immediately. It worked like a charm, and before she knew it, his manhood was standing at attention like a soldier. He lay down on the floor as she climbed on top of him, taking in every inch. Beautiful tried to run, but Todd grabbed her by the hips. "Don't you run from me."

"Yes, Daddy! Give it to me harder!"

And he did, until they both came.

CHAPTER 13

It was 8:00 the next morning. Todd awoke to the clatter of pots and pans. He rolled out of bed and put on his boxers to go down and see what all the commotion was about. When he opened the bedroom door, he saw Beautiful standing over the stove, scrambling eggs and frying bacon.

"Good morning," she said, smiling from ear to ear.

"Good morning, baby girl. Damn, you got it smelling good in here. What all you cooking?" he asked while rubbing the sleep out of his eyes.

"Eggs, bacon, toast, and grits. Did you want anything in particular?"

"No. I'll eat whatever you cook."

"Baby, you was talking in your sleep last night."

"Oh yeah? What did I say?"

"Something about respect."

They both started laughing.

"Well, I'm going in here to take a shower. I have a big day ahead of me." He went over to check the calendar on the refrigerator to confirm the date. Sure enough, it was Thursday, July 5. Todd had planned to pay Mac-9 a surprise visit, because he was still unaware of Money Mac's and Grip's murders. He looked over at the clock on the wall and saw that it was 8:10. Visitation didn't start until 8:30, so he had a little time. "Beautiful, when you get finished, get dressed, because I have to drop you off and go visit my uncle in prison."

"You got an uncle in prison?"

"Well, he's not really my uncle, but he was a close friend of my father's."

"Okay. Where do you keep the towels?"

"There're three new ones in the bathroom upstairs, on the right."

"Okay, Daddy."

"Oh yeah. I forgot to tell you that your sex is the bomb."

She smiled as he turned around and walked out of the kitchen.

Before getting in the shower, Todd stood in the mirror, rubbing his fingers up and down his chest and six-pack. Every since he'd stopped eating red meat and pork, he'd gotten skinny. "Damn! I'm losing weight," he said to himself, then hopped in the shower.

* * *

"Last call for big yard!" a dull voice yelled over the loud-speaker.

All the inmates at Wilcox State Prison began exiting their rooms and headed for the big yard to work out, run, and play basketball. The yard was surrounded by razor-wire fence, and there was a concrete basketball court, some pull-up bars, and a volleyball net hanging over red dirt. The inmates exited their housing units, and an officer in a blue uniform checked their names off of a roster sheet to take a headcount.

"Say, Mac-9, how many push-ups we starting off with?" Li'l Mark asked, taking off his shirt.

"Fifty. Then we going to super set with twenty pull-ups on the bar."

"That's what I like to hear!"

Mac-9 shook his head when he saw how excited Li'l Mark got when it came to working out.

* * *

Li'l Mark was only nineteen and stood at five-three. He was brown-skinned with a fit frame and a shiny bald head that stayed glossy, like a waxed floor. Having grown up in one of the most violent projects in Atlanta, Summer Hill, Li'l Mark thought he was unstoppable.

At the age of eighteen, he had been sentenced to life in prison for the death of his best friend, CB. Living the rich life in the city of Atlanta had caused CB to develop envy toward Li'l Mark, to the point where he'd started stealing money from him. Li'l Mark felt betrayed by the person he'd trusted the most, so he shot and killed CB as he was coming out of a store, right there in broad daylight.

While serving time in the Georgia Department of Corrections prison system, Mac-9 took a liking to Li'l Mark, because he reminded him so much of how he'd once been, growing up in the streets.

Li'l Mark had once been a member of the Bloods, but he'd slowly pulled away from that after Mac-9 embraced him like a son and taught him the true meaning of being a leader.

* * *

Mac-9 grabbed the pull-up bar and began doing his reps, while Li'l Mark did push-ups.

"Mr. Jones Douglas, report to visitation! Mr. Jones Douglas, report to visitation!" the voice called over the loudspeaker.

"That's you they calling for visitation," said Li'l Mark, dusting dirt from his pants.

Mac-9 looked surprised. "I wonder who it could be. I haven't had a visit since my mother passed away in 2008."

"Maybe it's your lawyer."

"On a Saturday? I doubt that. Mr. Adams only comes during the week, and I know it can't be my partners. They don't do the prison visit thing. They only send money orders." Mac-9 put his shirt back on. "Keep doing your thing, li'l homie. Let me go see who came to see the Mac."

Li'l Mark gave him some dap. "Okay. Have a good one."

* * *

After Todd dropped Beautiful off at Clark Atlanta, he stopped by his mother's crib and found a note she'd written, hanging on the front door:

Baby,

I waited up for you to come eat breakfast, but I have to make a few runs before the sun get too hot, and you know how I am about heat! LOL! But anyway, I cooked your favorite—pancakes, eggs, and grits. You may have to warm it up in the microwave. I should be back around 7:30 p.m. Don't forget to lock up when you leave. Oh yeah, I almost forgot. Cristal came by looking for you last night around 10:00. She said she wants you to call her. Well, I love you and will see you later.

Love,

Mama

SCHOOL BOY

He placed the letter in his pocket, got in his truck, and pulled off.

* * *

The visitation room at Wilcox State Prison was filled to capacity. The visitors were mostly African-Americans and Hispanics, sprinkled here and there with a few whites. Some of the women wore their best clothing, while others were dressed like they just didn't care. The younger children ran rampant, playing and happy to see their fathers or uncles for the first time in years.

Todd was wearing a white Polo shirt, white jeans, and a white Atlanta fitted cap that rested on top of his freshly done braids. He was draped in jewelry. He loved how he dressed himself, and many of the women stared him up and down, even though they were there to see their husbands and boy-friends. He even noticed one lady looking over at him while helping an inmate masturbate. Todd quickly turned his head and smiled. This shit here is wild.

He sat at a table in the far right corner of the visitation room, out of view of the correctional officers and guards.

The inmates were dressed in white, with blue stripes going down the side, and black boots. Though the clothes were really gaudy, most of the guys still tried to look their best for visitation.

Mac-9 finally came walking through the gray steel door, looking around the room. He was still short, with a brown-skinned complexion, a bald head, and a neatly trimmed goatee that was totally against regulations. Most of the correctional officers respected Mac-9 because of the outstanding conduct he displayed around the prison, though, so they didn't harass him about his goatee.

Todd spotted him standing in front of the drink machine and began walking toward him. "What's good, old man?"

Mac-9 turned around, and his eyes lit up like a candle when he saw Todd standing there. "Oh shit! Todd? Is that you, li'l nigga?"

"In the flesh."

Mac-9 quickly embraced him in a tight hug.

"You two have to take a seat at your table," said the young female correctional officer.

"I am the inmate, not him."

"Well, he can stand, but you need to sit down."

"Everything's all good, pretty lady," Todd smoothly replied, holding on to a plastic Ziploc filled with quarters.

She smiled and walked toward her desk.

"Do you want anything out of this vending machine?"

"Yeah. Get a few sandwiches, soda, and some chips."

Within minutes, Todd was walking to the table with the food.

Mac-9 immediately started eating like it was his last meal. "So, what brings you to the neck of these woods? How're Money and Grip?" he asked between bites.

Todd looked toward the floor, then glanced back up at Mac-9. "That's what I came to talk to you about."

Mac-9 stopped chewing. "What are you saying? Or should I say, what are you trying to say?"

Todd cleared his throat. "My dad and Grip are dead."

A serious look appeared on Mac-9's face, and he quickly jumped to his feet. The chair fell to the floor hard, and everyone turned their attention toward him and Todd, staring at them uncomfortably.

"How in the fuck did that happen? Do you know who did it?"

"Yeah."

"Yeah? You mean to tell me this nigga is still breathing?"

"Not for long."

A heavyset correctional officer with huge, ape-like hands walked up behind Mac-9. "What seems to be the problem, inmate Douglas?"

"There's no problem, Officer Hill."

"You know you've gotta take your seat before my lieutenant comes in here."

Mac-9 wanted to tell him to fuck off, but he knew that would only create more problems in his life, so he sat back down and held back his tears.

The correctional officer walked back over to the wooden desk.

Todd leaned over the table. "I killed one of the nigga's people last night. Trust me, I got the nigga who did it right where I want him. He won't be breathing long."

"Listen to me, young blood. You do what need to be done, but be careful. Once you become a killer, there's no walking away. Trust me…I know! And always clean up after yourself. That way, no evidence can lead them to you or no one you're fucking with." He leaned back in his seat. "How's your money looking?"

"Me, Hakim, and Chris are eating good. My dad left me straight for life."

"Good. You be the thinker and keep your eyes open."

"Check! I want you to know that I am going to support you while you're behind these walls."

Mac-9 gave him some dap over the table, and they sat and

talked until visitation time was over.

* * *

When Todd got back to his truck, he looked at his cell phone. There were five missed calls from Hakim and a text message that read: Get at me ASAP. Todd called Hakim with speed dial, and Hakim answered on the first ring.

"Bro, what it do?" Todd asked, pulling out of the prison parking lot.

"I called you like five times. Where you been?"

"I'm just leaving from Wilcox State Prison."

"Prison? Who at a prison?"

"Mac-9."

"Oh, okay. But peep the move, shawty. I don't like talking reckless over the phone, so come by my house when you get to the city."

"More good news?"

"You got to know that."

"Okay. Give me a few hours. I should be back in the city then."

"Bet that. I'm here."

"All right, one."

Todd hung up, rolled down all four windows, and cruised down the highway.

* * *

Three hours later, Todd was pulling into Hollywood Court Apartments, listening to Gucci Mane's "Back to the Trap House." He was reclined in the driver seat, with one hand clutching the oak wood steering wheel, feeling as if the world belonged to him. Everything Mac-9 had said to him was now a part of his motivation to get MT out of the way.

Just as he was about to park, his cellular rang. "Hello?"

"Hey there, baby boy," said Beautiful. "What you doin'?"

"Nothing much. Just pulling up at Hakim's spot."

"Tell me why this nigga MT called my phone saying police found his cousin Grady's body, burned to death."

Todd smiled. "Damn. That's fucked up."

"He said he knew who did it and that his people put a reward on the dude."

"Who did he say the dude is?"

"He didn't tell me. He just started laughing and hung up the phone in my face."

"Okay. That's what's up. Let me handle this business. I will call you later."

"Okay, but be careful. Love you."

"Love you too."

Todd ran into Hakim's apartment to give him the news. When he got to the living room, he found Hakim and Kee-Kee lying on the sofa, watching Bad Girls Club. "Shawty, let me talk to you," Todd said, standing in front of the television.

Hakim got up, and the walked into the kitchen. "What's up, bro?"

"Beautiful just called me saying that MT knows about his cousin being murdered."

"So what?"

"The nigga claim he know who did it, and he put a reward out."

"Damn!" Hakim said, sitting down at the table to think.

Todd started pacing back and forth. "I know who told that nigga."

"Who?" Hakim asked.

"That nigga you get your info from."

"Who? T-Man?"

"Hell yeah."

"Bro just told me today where MT laying his head. That's why I called you earlier."

"Do you trust him?"

"Yeah. Shawty keep it 100 with me. Stop overreacting. That lame could just be trying to pick her brain, to see what she knows."

"Let's pay this nigga a visit tonight. I want his blood."

Hakim looked down at his watch and saw that it was 8:00 p.m. He drew in a breath, then exhaled slowly. "Before we take care of old boy, I gotta meet Chris over on Sells Avenue so we can get off these three bricks."

"Okay. While y'all doing that, I'ma go to the house to change clothes. We'll meet back here around 10:00 p.m."

"All right."

"Shawty, why won't you and Kee-Kee move into a house? We making good money."

"This place is where it all started. I don't care how much money I get, I'll never leave my 'hood."

"If you say so," Todd said before he made his way to the front door.

When he opened it, Cristal was reaching for the doorknob, and the two of them jumped at the same time. "Damn, Todd! You scared me."

"Shit! You got me jumping too. Where you going looking all sexy tonight with that short dress on?"

She blushed. "Me and Kee-Kee going to Central Station to party. What is it to you anyway? You don't call or check up on me."

"I'm busy as hell."

"So you too busy to know that I'm pregnant?"

Todd looked surprised. "What you mean, you're pregnant?"

She placed her hand on her hips. "Me and Kee-Kee went to the doctor."

Todd glanced back at Kee-Kee and Hakim. "So y'all knew this?"

"Keep us out of it. That's y'all's business," said Kee-Kee.

"How come you haven't told me?"

"I went by your mother's house."

"What did the doctor say?"

"I am four weeks pregnant. Aren't you happy?"

"I am very happy, but I'm surprised. I got your back. Come here and give me a hug."

She stepped into the apartment and held Todd tightly.

* * *

The sound of car doors closing echoed through the half-empty parking lot of T.G.I. Friday's in Gainesville, Georgia. Hakim and Chris waited in the front with three kilos of cocaine under the passenger seat of Hakim's gold Range Rover. They were both armed with .45 handguns, resting on their laps.

Hakim glanced at his watch. It was 9:25 p.m., and already his prospective customer was late. "Do you think we oughtta get the hell outta here?" he asked.

"What time is it?"

"It's 9:26 p.m. on my watch."

"Let's wait another five minutes," Chris said, looking over his shoulder and scanning the parking lot.

"I don't like being up here with all this shit on me. Them damn Hispanic mother-fuckers better come on."

The Hispanics were never late when it came to doing business with Hakim and Chris, and Hakim was always on point for whatever came his way, but he knew how Gainesville was when it came to selling drugs. The police always rode around looking for a reason to use their weapons on anyone who got caught slipping. Getting caught with drugs in Gainesville was like killing a police officer in front of the police station.

Chris turned to Hakim. "Yeah, I feel you on that. Let's get the fuck outta here."

Just as Hakim started the ignition, a blue Lexus with chrome rims pulled up beside them.

Chris and Hakim recognized the Hispanic immediately. They rolled down the driver window, and the heavyset Mexican asked them to follow him.

Nervously, Hakim and Chris both looked around the parking lot before they followed the Lexus. About a half-mile later, they were pulling into a run-down apartment complex. Hispanic kids were running up and down the dirt road, playing. There wasn't a black person in sight.

The heavyset Mexican sprang out of the Lexus and signaled for Hakim and Chris to come in behind him with the drugs.

Hakim placed his pistol in his back pocket, and Chris put his in his waistband, then grabbed the three kilos.

Once they were inside the apartment, they felt there was no immediate danger. A short Hispanic woman was sitting at a wooden table, placing red and green rubber bands around the stacks of money that sat in front of her.

"Rosa, these are my friends, Hakim and Chris," the Mexican said in perfect English.

She nodded and smiled without taking her eyes off the money.

"Do you all have the shit, my friends?"

Chris held the three bricks of cocaine up. "It's right here."

"You said $28,000 a key, right?"

"All day. We keep that good shit, my Mexican friend," Hakim said.

"Ayo, Rosa! Give them the money and grab the work, mami."

Chris walked over to the table and handed Rosa the three kilos. She placed the cash in a small digital money machine, and he watched the numbers on the screen add up to $84,000. When Chris saw that the numbers added up correctly, he looked over at Hakim and nodded.

Hakim extended his hand to give the Mexican a powerful handshake.

"Good doing business with you, my friend," said the Mexican.

Chris raked the money into a black bag that Rosa had given him, and they left.

Back in the truck, Hakim's phone rang. He looked at the screen and saw that it was a restricted call, so he ignored it. When the phone rang again, he answered it in an angry tone. There was nothing on the end but heavy breathing, so he hung up.

* * *

Central Station nightclub was buzzing with activity. After waiting in line for nearly thirty-five minutes, Kee-Kee and Cristal finally made it to the front door.

The bodybuilder-looking security guard looked at Kee-Kee and Cristal with a strange expression on his face. "Hold on, you two. Show me your ID. Y'all look pretty young."

"Are you serious?" Kee-Kee said.

"Yes. This is my job, and I take it very seriously."

Cristal smiled, shaking her head. When she showed her ID, he let her walk through the glass doors.

Kee-Kee was still fumbling around in her purse, and then she realized she'd left her ID in the car. "Damn! I forgot my ID in the car."

The security guard smiled. "Go on and get it. I'll let you come back to the front."

Cristal stepped back out the door, looking confused. "What's wrong, Kee-Kee?"

"Girl, I left my ID card in the car."

Cristal looked at the security guard. "My girl is above the age. Let her come in this time."

"Rules are rules. I treat everybody equal."

"Girl, it's all good. I can go get it."

"Do you want me to come with you?"

"Naw, girl! Just wait for me at the bar. I'll be there in a minute."

"Okay."

* * *

The sound of Kee-Kee's high heels click-clacking against the pavement echoed through the parking lot of Lee's Detail Shop, which was across the street from Central Station nightclub. When she unlocked the door of her new Chrysler 300, a huge hand wrapped tightly over her mouth, and her eyes stretched wide. She glanced to her right, praying that someone might come by, but it was late and dark, and the lot was empty.

Kee-Kee looked in the reflection of the driver window and saw a man with a ski mask on, revealing only his mouth. Her eyes were filled with terror as she struggled to get loose from his grip. She felt his hot breath on the back of her neck.

"Bitch! You gon' die, just like that boyfriend of yours is," the masked man said in her ear. He wrapped his hands around her neck and began squeezing the life out of her.

Kee-Kee reached behind her and dug her fingernails into his eyes.

He immediately released his grip, and she took advantage of the situation by kicking him in the crotch.

The masked man fell to the ground like timber.

Kee-Kee reached in her purse and pulled out a can of pepper spray "This is for trying to choke me, mother-fucker!" She sprayed him in the eyes.

He started screaming like a woman.

Minutes later, Cristal came running through the lot, but she slowed down when she saw Kee-Kee standing over the man with a .380 pistol in her hand. "Kee-Kee!" she yelled.

Kee-Kee quickly pointed the gun at Cristal but lowered it when she realized who it was.

"What's going on, girl?"

"This piece of shit tried to kill me."

"Put the gun down and let's get out of here!"

"Yeah, put the gun down," the masked man said.

"Fuck you, nigga!" Kee-Kee screamed then pulled the trigger. She emptied the whole clip into the man's face and chest, and then she and Cristal jumped into the car and sped off.

Cristal was in the passenger seat, shaking like a leaf.

Kee-Kee fired up the blunt from the ashtray, trying to calm her nerves.

"Girl, you killed that man!"

Kee-Kee snapped, "Bitch, he tried to kill me! He said he was gonna kill me like he was gonna kill Hakim. I don't know who that nigga was, but something ain't right."

"I just haven't seen anyone get killed before."

"Well, you better get used to it. This is the real world, not some college story. Here. Hit this shit and pass me my phone out of the glove compartment."

Cristal passed Kee-Kee the phone before she inhaled the smoke.

When Kee-Kee called Hakim, it went straight to voicemail. She tried calling Todd and Chris, but she didn't have any luck with them either. "Damn it!" she said, slamming her phone down.

* * *

Todd, Hakim, and Chris were dressed in all black, staking out MT's house across the street. They were sitting in a black Suburban with dark-tinted windows in the Decatur area, a middle-class neighborhood populated with whites, blacks,

Hispanics, and Arabs who owned their own businesses.

All the lights in the house were on, and the shadow of four men walking back and forth in the living room displayed through the window like a movie scene.

Before moving in, Todd wanted to make sure MT was in the house. They could have just driven by and shot the entire house up, but Todd felt that would have been too sloppy. He wanted to make sure the bullet that killed MT would come straight from his gun.

MT's red Dodge Viper and 2012 Chrysler were parked in the front yard. A white BMW drove up with a young black man behind the wheel, smoking a cigarette. He blew the horn twice, and MT came out of the house and walked up to the vehicle with a briefcase in his hand.

Todd smiled, looking over at Hakim in the passenger seat, gripping on a sixteen-shot shotgun. Chris checked the chamber of his M-16 and made sure his bulletproof vest was strapped on tight.

After MT passed the young man in the BMW the briefcase, he walked back into the house and closed the door behind him. The BMW sped off, music blaring loudly from the stereo.

"Let's get this show on the road!" said Todd, jumping out of the Suburban with the twin Glock .45s in his hand. "I'ma go around to the back of the house. Hakim, you and Chris kick the front door in."

"How will we know when?" Chris asked.

"Just wait for my signal. You'll know. Trust me."

Todd slowly crept up the stairs of the wooden deck with his hands gripping his pistols tightly. He moved like a professional hit man. The sliding glass door was open a crack, and the vertical blinds were pulled back. Todd could hear a female's voice in the kitchen, so he peeked in.

Beautiful was standing over the counter with a glass of Ace of Spades champagne in her hand. She was wearing skin-tight capri pants and a blue midriff shirt that revealed a hint of her belly.

Todd couldn't believe his eyes. The woman he'd been willing to give his heart to was standing right there in the house of his enemy. "This bitch!" he mumbled, reaching for the door handle.

MT walked into the kitchen, smiling from ear to ear.

Todd quickly stepped back to the side, keeping his pistols positioned to open fire.

MT kissed Beautiful's lips, and she wrapped her arms around his neck, staring into his eyes.

Todd watched, thinking of killing them both, but a voice startled him. He quickly turned around with his pistols pointed and saw that it was Hakim.

MT heard movement outside the window and walked to the back deck. He looked around but didn't see anyone, so he stepped back inside, locking the sliding door behind him.

Todd and Hakim crawled out from under the deck and began walking back to the truck.

"Let's ride, Chris," Hakim said, walking beside Todd and trying to figure out why they were leaving without killing MT.

When they all got into the Suburban, Todd rested his head on the steering wheel, wishing that his whole life was one big dream.

"Are we just going to sit here?" Hakim asked after staring out the window, into the dark woods.

Without responding, Todd started the engine and pulled off.

CHAPTER 14

The date was July 6, 2012, and the sun was at its highest, at 106 degrees. DeKalb County police had the streets blocked off with wooden barriers, and yellow crime scene tape surrounded the beautiful luxury two-story split-level house. It wasn't common for there to be so much criminal activity in that integrated neighborhood, so the street was packed with curious neighbors, news reporters, and a group of detectives who were walking around and asking questions.

Inside the house, a tall, brown complexion, bald detective stared down into the waxy face of a young man, approximately in his early twenties, lying dead on the living room floor. Beside him was another black male in his mid-thirties, lying in a fetal position with his hands clutching his stomach and blood seeping through the cracks between his teeth. The detective looked over at the four boxes of pizza lying on the coffee table, then glanced at the four glasses of champagne. There was red lip gloss around the rim of one. He pulled out a pair of latex gloves from his jacket pocket and threaded them over his fingers. As he picked the glass up, he closely examined it for fingerprints.

Upstairs in the master bedroom, two detectives stood over the body of another young man, lying face down across the bed. Next to him, they found an empty champagne glass, an ounce of crack cocaine in a plastic Ziploc bag, and a .357 revolver.

One of the detectives reached on the bed and grabbed the lifeless body, then turned the head around. A surprised look came over his face. "I know this kid," said the detective.

The other detective moved in closer to get a better look of his face. "Yeah, that's Michael Tayler, aka MT." The detective grabbed the bag of crack cocaine. "Well, we know it's drug related, but what's the cause of death?"

"I think I know that too." The detective walked toward the door and picked up a very small, clear container. He put it up to his nose and smelled the strange aroma that lingered from the bottle. "Snake venom. These guys were poisoned."

* * *

The clock on the wall read 2:30 p.m. Hakim lay across the hotel room bed with the remote control in his hand, searching for the evening news. After Todd had dropped him and Chris off in Hollywood Court, Kee-Kee and Cristal had pulled up in a panic.

Kee-Kee had immediately told Hakim about the incident in the Lee's Detail Shop parking lot. Hakim was already frustrated with Todd because of the way he'd abandoned their mission, and after what he heard from Kee-Kee, he was sure MT had the upper hand and knew their every move. Todd never told Hakim or Chris why he didn't want to complete the mission. For the whole drive, Todd had remained silent, keeping his thoughts to himself.

Without thinking twice, Hakim told Chris to drop Cristal off at her house, and then he and Kee-Kee had checked into a hotel outside of Atlanta so he could be safe while he figured out what was really going on.

On the local Channel 2 news, photos of MT and his two cousins flashed across the screen. The anchorman called MT a "known drug dealer" and said he'd been "found in his two-story split-level home."

Hakim quickly grabbed his cell phone off the pillow and dialed Todd's number. After the phone rang four times, Todd answered in a sleepy voice. "Brah, you still asleep?" Hakim asked, smiling from ear to ear.

"Yeah. What time is it?"

"It's 2:39 p.m. You think you're slick too, brah."

"Why you say that?"

"It's all over the news."

Todd sat up in bed. "What's on the news?"

"That nigga MT is dead, and it's all over the news. Where did you go after you dropped us off?"

"Shawty, stop playing. It's too early for the games."

"Games! Turn on your TV on Channel 2 news."

"Hold on."

"Okay."

Todd grabbed the remote control off the nightstand and turned the television on. As soon as he turned it to Channel 2, a picture of MT's face was posted in the far right corner of the screen. Then, an old gray-haired detective in a blue business suit stepped in front of the camera and stated that the case was being viewed as a homicide, but no further information would be given out until the investigation was complete.

Todd sat at the edge of the bed, wondering if Beautiful was still in the house when MT and his cousins were murdered. If she was, he thought, that means the murderer let her leave. It must have been someone she knew!

Todd placed the phone back against his ear. "Hello?"

"I'm still here. Did you see what I'm talking about?"

"Yeah. Someone else killed that nigga, brah, and that's on my father's grave. I didn't do it."

"I believe you. That nigga had some enemies. But anyway, fuck that nigga. He's out of the picture now."

Todd forced a smile, still thinking that Beautiful was somehow involved. "Brah, you at the house?" he asked.

"Hell naw. Oh, I didn't tell you. Me and Kee-Kee had to get a room because some nigga at the club last night tried to kill her in the parking lot."

"What the fuck?"

"Yeah. She shot the nigga though."

"This shit is crazy. Who do you think the nigga was?"

"One of MT's people, because Kee-Kee said the nigga told her he was gon' kill her man after he killed her. Shawty, you know just like I know that we didn't have any enemies but MT."

"Yeah, you're right."

"I am happy the fuck nigga is dead. That's one less nigga we gotta worry about. I got your part of the money from the drop we made with the Mexican, by the way."

"Nigga, what are you doing with all this money we giving you?"

Todd smirked. "Saving up until I get this club."

"That bitch gon' be jumping. Well, me and Kee-Kee decided to move out of the 'hood and into a house finally."

"Oh yeah? What made y'all decide on that?"

"Brah, she wants to have a baby, and I refuse to raise mine in the 'hood around crack-heads, gangsters, and cut-throat mother-fuckers."

"I feel that! When my kid and your kid come into this world, we'll be rich."

"Damn right! Well, Kee-Kee is getting out of the shower. I'll see you later. Oh, before we hang up, tell me…why did we abandon that mission last night?"

"I felt like it wasn't the right time," Todd lied, not wanting to let Hakim know that Beautiful was inside MT's house.

"Okay. Well, that's what's up. Get at me later."

"Check that."

Hakim hung up the phone, then lay back on the bed with a huge smile on his face. He felt relieved now that MT was out of the picture.

Minutes later, Kee-Kee came out of the bathroom with a white robe on and a towel wrapped around her head. "So, when can we start workin' on that baby?" she asked.

* * *

Todd lay wide awake in bed, listening to the rain pelting the roof. It died down after about twenty minutes, but then the sound of a car engine pulling in his driveway alerted his awareness. He quickly grabbed his pistol from under the pillow and ran to the living room window to look out. He saw a red Escalade SUV, and when the driver door popped open, Beautiful climbed out, wearing a black raincoat.

When Beautiful stepped up on the porch, Todd opened the door. He had a wide smile on his face. She smiled back as she walked through the door and removed the wet coat. Todd grabbed it and placed it on the coat rack beside the window.

The blue dress she was wearing fit her petite frame well.

Her hair was once again short, and the black eyeliner was smeared down her cheeks like she'd been crying.

Todd looked down at her hands and noticed they were shaking. A feeling of nervousness overwhelmed his thought process, and he slowly eased his hand on his pistol. Todd didn't know what to expect of her after hearing that MT and his cousins were found dead. The thoughts in his mind left him on edge. He wondered who she really was and what her intentions were in popping up at his house unannounced. With his hand under his shirt, he spoke. "So what brings you out this way?" he asked, examining her every move.

She stared at the floor for a second, then looked up at Todd. "I have a confession to make, and you may not like it."

Todd peeked out the window to make sure there weren't any surprise guests. The sky had darkened, and the rain had begun to pour down hard. If she was trying to set him up or have him killed, it would have been the perfect time, because he couldn't see a thing outside. "Hold on before you tell me." He walked over to the door and locked both locks. "Okay. I'm ready for whatever you've got to say."

"I killed MT and his cousins last night," she said, and tears began to stream down her face.

"What?" he quickly yelled, pretending to be angry. "I mean…why?"

"I knew you wouldn't understand."

"No! I'm listening. Keep talking," he coaxed, still peeking out the window.

"See? You don't trust me."

"Why do you say that?"

"That's the second time you've looked out the window."

Todd cleared his throat. "Finish telling me why you killed

MT."

"He kept calling my phone, leaving threats about killing you."

Todd leaned against the wall, tightly gripping his pistol. He wanted to believe what Beautiful was saying, because he really did love her, but believing that she killed MT to protect him was too much for him to take in. After all, they'd only had sex one time. He wanted to tell her he'd seen her and MT kissing, but he knew that would have exposed his hand, so he decided to keep it to himself. "You mean to tell me that you killed MT for me?"

She nodded.

"I want to know how you did it. MT and his cousins had guns on them at all times."

She wiped the tears from her eyes with the back of her hand, then walked over to the bar and grabbed a bottle of E&J Brandy from the glass shelf. She took a quick drink from the bottle before speaking. "It was simple. I told him we would be together only if he promised to love me the right way. He agreed and came to pick me up at the college. Then I—"

"Hold up!" Todd said, cutting her off as he thought about what she was telling him. "Who all knew you were going over to MT's house?"

"No one. I didn't even tell my best friend Peaches."

"Okay. Go on."

"I wasn't expecting his cousins to be there, but they were. I asked everyone if they wanted a glass of Ace of Spades champagne, because they'd already been drinking before we got there. They all wanted some, so I went in the kitchen and poured everyone some. I added poisonous snake venom to theirs."

Todd smiled. "Were you scared?"

She took another drink from the bottle. "I was terrified. MT almost caught me. I had to kiss him when I didn't want to."

Todd now knew she was telling him the truth. He eased his hand off the gun and walked over to her. "Come here and give me a hug. You are safe now, my queen. No one knows of this but you and me."

She set the bottle down and embraced him. "Baby, why do you have a gun on you?" she asked.

"There's so much happening around here, and I've got to protect myself."

"I understand, Todd. I love you!"

"I love you too. Let's get you out of this wet dress before you get sick."

She pushed the blouse down over her naked breasts and stepped out of the blue sundress, nude. Her body was magnificent, smooth, slender, and buxom all at the same time.

Todd removed his pistol and laid it on top of the counter. He then picked Beautiful up and carried her to the bedroom. He unbuttoned his shirt and struggled awkwardly out of it, then pulled off his shoes and socks. Next, he removed his underwear, and she knelt on the end of the bed and worked her lips up and down his thigh, then took hold of him lovingly and caressed him with her tongue. It took only seconds before he exploded in her mouth.

"Oh, baby, you taste good," she stated, licking the head of his penis.

Todd smiled, then lay back on the bed, feeling a million times better than before.

She climbed onto the bed and lay beside him. "Now me,"

she whispered.

He rolled on top of her, and she wrapped her legs around his waist like a hula hoop.

He slowly eased his penis inside of her wetness, and she gripped his back with her fingernails. As he ground in and out of her, she began to forget about the harsh feelings she had toward men. Todd was everything she could have ever wanted, a real man, and she was willing to do whatever it took to keep him.

CHAPTER 15

It had been nearly two years since the murder of MT and his cousins, and life was going great for Todd. He'd finally graduated from Clark Atlanta with his business degree and was ready to move on with his life. The half-million dollars his father had left in the Will was now in his possession for him to spend on his new nightclub he'd built in Buckhead.

Two days before his twenty-sixth birthday, Cristal had given birth to a five-pound, healthy baby boy. Since it was Todd's first, he named him Quontavious Jackson Jr.

Cristal also graduated with her computer programming degree and started working for the Microsoft Corporation in New York City. After she'd seen Kee-Kee kill a man in cold blood, she'd decided she wanted to live a different lifestyle, with or without Todd. At first, Todd wouldn't allow her to move to New York, where she had no friends, but she later convinced him to let her live her own dreams. They both agreed that Quontavious should be raised in New York City, where he could receive a better education and an opportunity to see a greater place than Atlanta. Todd promised to visit from time to time, until Cristal moved back to Georgia.

As far as Beautiful, Todd made her change careers and enroll in forensic sciences, so she could learn the processing of crime scenes and the fundamentals of DNA analysis. Even though she was hurt about Todd's baby, she still cared for him unconditionally.

Hakim and Chris were now doing big business with the Mexican cartel in Gainesville. They were moving pounds of cocaine throughout the Atlanta district. Even Jay-Bo and GG had started purchasing work from them because of the long drought that had taken place after Money's death.

* * *

It was 5:30 p.m., and the sun began to set. Chris and his son Wāhid sat in the living room of their new mansion, playing Xbox, while Monica stood in the kitchen with the maid, preparing supper. Now that he was a big-time hustler, he and his family had everything they had ever wanted or dreamt of. From the luxury cars to the expensive jewelry, life was a paradise.

"Wāhid, go in the kitchen and help Mama while Daddy smoke his medicine," Chris said, reaching under the luxurious leather sofa and pulling out a golden tray filled with high-grade marijuana.

Wāhid got up from the marble floor and ran toward the kitchen playfully.

Chris fired up the blunt while staring up at the golden chandelier hanging from the ceiling. All of the sudden, a sharp pain shot through his leg, and the blunt fell from his fingers. He quickly clutched his shin.

Wāhid looked up at him with an innocent expression. He had bumped into his father's leg with his toy truck.

Chris grabbed the burning blunt off the arm of the sofa

and laid it in the ashtray. "Come here, little big-head boy! You trying to hurt me?" When he reached down to grab his son, a swift breeze zoomed past his head. He quickly looked back and saw a small hole in the wall. He glanced over at the four security monitors and saw that five fully armed intruders, dressed in all black, were creeping over the twelve-foot brick wall that surrounded the mansion.

Chris immediately reached under the cushion of the corner wedge couch and pulled out a chrome-plated AK-47 rifle. He then yelled for Monica.

Within seconds, she came running through the living room with her cooking apron still wrapped around her small waist. She quickly stopped, and a surprised look came over her face when she saw Chris putting a bullet into the chamber.

"Don't just stand there! Get Wāhid and go down in the basement."

She was puzzled. "What's wrong?"

Chris bit down on his bottom lip. "Stop asking questions and do what I say! Damn!"

Just as she took a step toward Wāhid, flying bullets shattered the glass sliding doors. She dived head first behind the left arm of the loveseat, and Chris jumped on top of his son, becoming a human shield. Bullets repeatedly flew past his head, missing him by mere inches.

When the shooting stopped, Chris stood to his feet and returned fire.

Wāhid cried at the top of his lungs, covering his ears with his hands.

Chris glanced down at his son and shouted, "Monica, get my son out of here!"

But there was no response.

He peeked around the loveseat and saw her lying on the floor, holding her stomach with both hands. Blood was gushing through her fingers, and her face grew pale as she fought to remain conscious.

Chris shook his head, and his eyes filled with rage and tears. "Don't you die on me."

She slightly smiled. Her eyes closed, then opened again.

Chris turned around to pick his son up, but bullets began coming at him from the front foyer, flying past at a tremendous rate of speed. With his free arm, he quickly scooped the boy up and ran toward the kitchen, where he found the maid hiding behind the counter with a sharp knife in her hand. He set Wāhid down, then motioned for her to come from behind the counter.

She stared blankly, then slowly started walking toward him.

"You have to move faster than that!"

"Look out behind you!" yelled the maid.

The loud cocking of the shotgun hit his adrenaline, and he swiftly turned around with his AK-47 pointed directly at the masked man. Chris fired multiple rounds into the intruder's flesh. The impact from the chopper bullets caused the intruder's body to jerk violently. "Ms. Rose, get my son down in the basement now!" Chris yelled.

The maid obliged and scrambled to the basement with the crying and frightened boy.

Three intruders came running through the kitchen with M-16 machineguns ready to open fire. When they saw Chris, the let the weapons rip without hesitation.

Chris quickly ran through the hallway and into the guest room. The sound of combat boots stomping against the well-polished marble floors came closer. Chris positioned himself in the center of the room, with the AK-47 aimed directly at the hallway. Who in the fuck are these guys, and why would they want to kill me? he thought. He knew they weren't professional killers, because they walked right past the room and were immediately gunned down like a group of untamed gorillas.

Chris wiped the sweat from his forehead, then walked into the hallway. The place looked a mess. Thick blood filled the corridor, and bullet holes had redesigned the walls. The horrible smell of death hovered in the air.

Two of the gunmen lay dead against the baseboard, while one struggled to crawl away.

Chris walked up behind the wounded gunman and snatched his ski mask off. "Turn your bitch ass over before I blow your mother-fucking head off your shoulders!"

The gunman did as he was told.

Chris had never seen him before, but the look on his face showed that he was terrified and in serious pain from the chopper bullets that had half amputated his leg. "Who are you? Who sent you to my house?"

"Fuck you, nigga!" the gunman said with a New Orleans accent.

Chris smirked. "Is that right?" He raised the AK-47 toward the gunman's head, then shot him twice in the face, scattering brain matter all over the floor and his own white t-shirt.

* * *

The golden, crystal-shaped chandelier hanging from the vaulted ceiling of Hakim's mansion lit the spacious front foyer like a luminous twenty-four-karat diamond gleaming in the sun. The loud music coming from the surround-sound echoed through the spacious hallways as Hakim and Kee-Kee counted $5 million in cash out in their luxury master bedroom. Living the lives of millionaires was a sign of their ambition toward a successful life.

Kee-Kee strolled toward the living room with a glass of expensive champagne in her hand. Her pink silk gym shorts and midriff, skin-tight shirt fit her petite frame perfectly. She looked down at the twenty-four-karat gold watch Hakim had given her for her birthday. It was 8:20 p.m.

The moon was full, and the sky was dark. The trees outside by the swimming pool swayed back and forth with the powerful wind.

Suddenly, the music stopped, and a loud bang at the front door startled her, to the point where she almost dropped her glass on the green marble floor.

Hakim came running through the hallway with two .45 Glocks in his hand. "Grab a gun from the closet! I saw it on the monitor. A Silverado truck rammed straight through our front gate!"

Without hesitation, Kee-Kee set the glass down on the coffee table and ran to the large closet. Within minutes, she came out with two Uzi machineguns, tightly in her grip.

Hakim walked over to the small circuit breaker mounted on the wall. "I want you to position yourself behind the kitchen steel door. When they come in, you shoot everything that's walking."

She nodded, then ran behind the door, keeping her Uzis ready to rip.

Hakim lowered the switch on the circuit breaker, and all

the lights shut down. It was pitch dark.

All of the sudden, infrared beams shone down on them from the top of the spiral staircase like a laser show.

Hakim and Kee-Kee began to panic. They weren't expecting the intruders to creep up on them through the top of the roof.

Hakim looked to his right and noticed two more intruders creeping through the living room. Not wanting to draw attention to Kee-Kee as she slowly crept toward the kitchen like a shadow in the dark, he fired a few rounds toward the intruders while they crept down the stairs.

One of the gunmen fell over the steel rail when the flying bullets penetrated his forehead. His body slammed into the marble floor like a ton of bricks, and heavy, thick blood poured from his head and mouth.

The other three gunmen standing on the stairs opened fire on Hakim, and the room lit up like the Fourth of July.

Just as Hakim turned the corner, the gunman creeping through the living room cut him off by placing the barrel of the gun to his temple. At that moment, he knew he'd been caught slipping, and there was nothing he could do. He slowly closed his eyes, knowing he was about to experience death without ever getting a chance to see his unborn child that Kee-Kee was carrying inside of her.

The strange gargle and silent scream caused him to panic. He quickly turned around and saw the gunman stumbling back with a sharp knife planted in his neck.

"Did you think I was going to let you go out bad like that?" Kee-Kee softly said, standing against the wall like a dark shadow.

Hakim smiled. "There're three more. You ready to get this

problem out of the way?"

"Baby, please. The way I move, you would have thought I was a professional at this shit. Let's get these niggas out of our house."

"Okay. Be careful."

Hakim was surprised to see his girl holding up the way she was. He was frightened himself, but the way Kee-Kee acted, he would have thought she was a cold-blooded killer.

She ran back through the kitchen while Hakim watched the gunmen give themselves away with the infrared beams that danced around the front room.

Hakim and Kee-Kee moved in on the gunmen, studying their every step and listening to their heavy breathing.

Kee-Kee stood in the doorway of the gym with both guns aimed at the intruders. She smiled and squeezed the trigger.

Before Hakim could let off a shot, the three gunmen were swimming in their own blood, with multiple bullet wounds in their bodies.

All of the sudden, the lights in the front foyer flashed back on.

Hakim glanced down at the gunmen. Their bodies were stacked on top of each other, with blood leaking from the exit wounds like a water faucet. He then looked around the room and saw Kee-Kee in front of the circuit breaker, smiling, with sweat dripping from her forehead.

* * *

It was half-past nine, and the night was just getting started for hundreds of women and men who were standing in line outside Cristal's Diamond Nightclub.

Todd stood behind the bulletproof, one-way mirror glass window of his plush, elevated office, admiring his great success. He'd had the elevated office built into the brick walls so that he would be able to see the entire club with his own eyes. He trusted no one but Hakim and Chris when it came to dealing with his money. The special designed Louis Vuitton suit fit his muscular frame well. He was draped in diamonds and jewelry, with two gun holsters strapped across each shoulder, just like his father used to wear. His long braids were neatly designed, and his goatee connected with his trimmed mustache. Todd looked like new money and was now living the life he'd always dreamt of. The only thing that was missing from his life was his father, Money Mac, who had taught him everything he'd needed to know about the streets and life itself.

Todd took a sip from the fresh bottle of Louis XII Rémy Martin brand. He then looked down at the crowd on the dance floor, who were having the time of their lives, grinding and grooving to Drake's new song, "Money to Blow."

The DJ dimmed the lights and announced over the microphone that he was about to slow the mood down with some slow jam music. Women and men began joining hands and doing the two-step.

Todd smiled, then went and sat behind his bowling-ball marble desk. He reclined in his leather chair and stared at the large picture on the wall of him, Cristal, and their son Quontavious.

The ringing of his phone interrupted his thoughts. Before answering, he let it ring twice. "Hello?"

"Mr. Jackson, you have visitors," said the bartender.

"Who is it?"

"I don't know, but I can tell they're not from around here."

"Hold on." Todd got up from his chair and walked over to the one-way glass. Standing in front of the horseshoe-shaped glass bar were three Italian men dressed in business suits, observing the crowd on the dance floor. The expressions on their faces showed that they were harmless, but Todd wasn't going to take any chances of allowing anyone to get close to him without him being on point.

He strolled back over to his desk, reached under it, and adjusted the double-barreled shotgun he had mounted to a roller just in case of emergencies. He then picked up the phone and told the bartender to send them up.

Within minutes, they were being escorted into the office by one of Todd's security guards.

The three gentlemen greeted Todd with a firm handshake, then stood exactly where he wanted them to stand: in front of his desk, where he had easy access to fire the double-barreled shotgun at him if necessary.

Todd took a seat behind his desk and grabbed hold of the shotgun. "So, what brings you gentlemen to my nightclub."

The tall, pecan-colored mobster removed his hat from his head. "First of all, Mr. Jackson, you can take your hand off that gun under your desk."

Todd looked surprised. "How did you know I was holding a gun? And why should I trust you all when I've never seen you before?"

"Come on, Mr. Jackson! That's one of the oldest tricks in the book. You have us stand in front of your desk while you hold on to your shotgun. It's textbook."

The other two mobsters laughed.

"If we wanted you dead, we would have never come to do

it ourselves. We have men for that job."

Todd removed his hand from under the desk, then sat back in his chair with his hand on his chin. "What business do we have, gentlemen?"

The tall mobster took another step closer to the desk. "Business? We're not here for business. We flew in from New York with a proposition for you."

"What kind of proposition would bring you guys to Georgia?"

The short, heavyset mobster cut in on the question. "Before we inform you, allow us to introduce ourselves. My name is Don Cornelious."

"My name is Don Gotti," said the tall mobster.

"And my name is Don Sapareno."

"Oh shit! You guys are the mob. So y'all are telling me I have three dons from three different families coming all the way from New York to talk with me?"

They nodded at the same time.

"But why?"

The short, heavyset mobster spoke. "We came for your father, but we found out later he is dead. A few years ago, he helped us out by killing a man by the name of Devon, and we never got a chance to thank him. If you are anything like your father was, we would like for you to join us."

Todd stood to his feet. "Join you?" He smiled. "How much money are we talking about, and what would my position be?"

"Have you ever dealt with heroin?"

"No, but I have two brothers who are familiar with selling it."

"Who? Hakim and Chris?"

"Damn! You know them" Todd asked, grabbing the bottle

of Louis from the desk.

"We know everything. Some of our friends work down at the FBI headquarters, and they ran your names for us. Mr. Jackson, there's nothing to worry about. Doctors, lawyers, judges, and federal agents are on our payroll. You will make millions. So what do you say?"

Todd looked over at the picture of his family on the wall and smiled. "I say we have a deal, under one condition."

They looked at each other, then spoke at the same time, "What?"

"Hakim and Chris join as well."

"Done!"

Todd walked around the desk and gave them all a vigorous handshake.

The heavyset mobster reached into his coat pocket and handed Todd a business card. "Contact us at the number on the card."

"Okay."

The three gentlemen walked out of the room, and Todd took a sip of Louis while he sat back in his chair, feeling excitement flow through his body.

Fifteen minutes after the mobsters left, Todd decided to head home. He opened the sliding drawer beneath his desk and retrieved his twin Glock .45s. He placed the guns in their holsters strapped to his shoulders, grabbed his dress coat from the rack next to the filing cabinet, then walked out the door.

Just as Todd was making his way through the large crowd, he glanced up at the VIP room on the second floor. There was a group of high-rollers yelling and screaming, popping expensive bottles of champagne. Todd just smiled, then walked over to the bar and handed the old gray-headed bartender the keys to lock up.

When he turned around to walk off, he noticed a caramel-skinned woman in a skin-tight dress, sitting at the bar with her back toward him. Todd was curious and wanted to know how beautiful she was in the face, so he slowly approached her while adjusting his silk tie. "Now why would a sexy woman such as yourself be sitting at the bar alone?" he whispered in her ear.

She slowly turned around on the barstool

Todd took a step back, and his eyebrows rose. A surprised look came over his handsome face. He tried to speak, but the words wouldn't come out.

The woman stood to her feet. "Todd? Is that you?" she asked, smiling from ear to ear.

Todd couldn't believe his eyes. His middle school class-mate, Gabrielle, stood right before him, looking like a beautiful angel sent from Heaven. "Yes. This is me."

She quickly hugged him. Her body felt like a soft pillow, and the fragrance from her neck smelled sweet.

He slowly closed his eyes as he whispered in her ear, "Gabrielle, where have you been all my life?"

She released her grip, then ran her fingers gently through his braids. "I've been going through an abusive marriage with my husband because I caught him cheating. I've recently filed for a divorce, and now I'm single, sitting at the bar, having a drink." She looked him up and down. "I see you're looking handsome in that suit. How's life been treating you?"

Todd grinned, then held his arms out. "All of this is mine!"

"This yo' club?" she asked with excitement in her voice.

"Yes…and drinks are on me." He hit the glass counter with the palm of his hand, and the bartender immediately walked over.

"You need me, Mr. Jackson?"

"Yes. This fine lady here is a great friend of mine. Make sure she gets whatever she needs—on the house."

"Will do, sir."

"Why thank you, Todd."

"Thank me by coming back so we can take a trip down memory lane."

"Okay. I can do that tomorrow night."

"Tony will make sure you get what you want. I'll talk to you tomorrow with your sexy ass."

She smiled, standing back up. As Todd strolled through the crowd, she watched him until he exited the double doors that led to his personal parking spot.

The security guards greeted him as he jumped in his blue 2012 Mercedes SIS AMG E-Cell.

* * *

An hour and a half later, he was pulling into the front gate of his mansion. He pressed the red button on his car steering wheel, and seconds later, the gate opened. He drove into the driveway and parked behind his Range Rover.

The time on the CD player read 1:40 a.m. Todd turned the engine off and climbed out of the car, then made his way to the front door.

When he walked in the front room, it was very dark. He reached over on the wall and flicked on the light switch. Todd quickly reached for his gun, but he was too slow on the draw.

Two masked gunmen was sitting at the bar with their guns aimed directly at his head and chest. "Um, I wouldn't do that if I was you," said one of the gunmen. "Slowly remove your hand from that handle, before I blow your fucking head clean off your shoulders."

Todd eased his hand away from the handle of the gun. "I've got money if that's what y'all want. Take what you want and let's call it a night. That way, no one gets hurt."

Both gunmen started laughing. "We're not here for your money."

One of the gunmen walked over to Todd, grabbed his guns from their holsters, and tossed them on the floor. He then patted Todd down, searching him from head to toe, and locked the two deadbolts on the front door. The gunman then escorted Todd into the kitchen, where he made him sit in a wooden chair, with his hands behind his back.

The other gunman walked into the kitchen with duct tape in his hand. He taped Todd's legs and arms to the chair, then stood in front of him, breathing heavily.

Todd stared at him, puzzled, then opened his mouth to speak.

The gunman aggressively backhanded Todd in the mouth, sending a spray of blood from his lips and causing his head to jerk backward.

The gunman who was the most aggressive removed his mask from his face. He had a long scar beneath his right eye. His skin was very dark, and his hair was like wool.

Todd looked at him closely, trying to figure out if he'd ever seen him before.

When the second gunman removed the mask, Todd's eyes grew wide.

"You're a…a girl!"

"Uh-huh. Do you have a problem with that?" she softly

asked, brushing her jet-black hair from her beautiful face.

"I offered you money and you don't want that, so I just want to know what I have done to deserve this."

The male gunman raised his hand to slap Todd again, but she grabbed his arm.

"Enough!" she yelled in a demanding voice.

He snatched his arm away from her grip, then walked into the living room with an attitude.

She grabbed a chair and placed it right in front of Todd. "I know you don't know me, but you remember my three brothers, right?"

"Who are they?"

She reached into her back pocket and pulled out a piece of paper and began to read. "On April 5, 1999, three brothers were found dead in a run-down shed with multiple gunshot wounds. Does that ring a bell?"

Todd had no idea what she was talking about, so he shook his head. "No."

An angry look appeared on her face, and she grabbed the gun from her waistband and aimed it right in the center of his forehead. "Meco, Rock, and AJ were my brothers, you mother-fucker! For years, I watched you from a distance."

Todd couldn't believe what he was hearing. His past had come to haunt him, and there was nothing he could do about it.

She started to laugh. "Don't you remember the white Lexus that slowly drove in front of you the night you and Chris were together? I'm talking about the night outside the Towers Liquor Store."

"What about it?"

Those guys who tried to kill you were my men. I almost

had you that night, but that store manager saved you."

He drew in a breath. "You killing me won't bring your brothers back."

She stood to her feet and began to pace the room. "You're right. It won't bring my brothers back, just like it won't bring your father back."

"What are you saying? What do you know about that?"

She smirked. "Before I killed your father, I stared him in the eyes."

Tears began to stream down Todd's face. "You didn't kill my father. MT did."

She laughed loudly. "That information came from me. I had the streets thinking MT was involved because I saw you two beefing over some ho. The poor man never even hurt a fly."

Everything she was saying began to weigh heavily on his mind, and sweat began to fall from his forehead. He suddenly didn't care if he lived or died, but he wanted to get back at her. "I'ma kill you, bitch!" Todd snapped as he tried to break free from the duct tape but only fell to the floor.

The Haitian-looking gunman ran into the kitchen with his gun drawn on Todd.

"Jean, I want his pinky!"

The Haitian smiled, then pulled a knife out of his pocket.

"Oh yeah, Todd, you killing me is not going to happen. When I get finished with you, I'll be in Miami on the beach, sipping some expensive wine with your finger around my neck as a souvenir."

The loud screaming echoed through the kitchen as the Haitian cut into Todd's little finger with the sharp knife. Blood poured from his hand like a busted water pipe, and the pain was almost unbearable.

She knelt down on one knee and whispered, "Your friends are also dead, and they are waiting on you in the afterlife."

"I will kill you."

She stood with her gun aimed to fire. "We'll see about that!" Her fingers squeezed the trigger, and five bullets entered Todd's chest.

His eyes slowly closed...